THE SHIP THAT VOTED NO
AND OTHER STORIES
OF SHIPS AND THE SEA

THE SHIP THAT VOTED NO AND OTHER STORIES OF SHIPS AND THE SEA

By Tony Keene

359
.00971
Kee

LANCELOT PRESS
Hantsport, Nova Scotia

ISBN 0-88999-588-5
Published 1995

All rights reserved. No part of this book may be reproduced in any form without written permission of the publisher except brief quotations embodied in critical articles or reviews.

ACKNOWLEDGEMENT: This book has been published with the assistance of the Nova Scotia Department of Education, Cultural Affairs Division and the Canada Council.

LANCELOT PRESS LIMITED, Hantsport, Nova Scotia
Office and production facilities situated on Highway No. 1,
1/2 mile east of Hantsport

Mailing Address:
P.O. Box 425, Hantsport, Nova Scotia B0P 1P0
Phone (902) 684-9129   Fax (902) 684-3685

Contents

The Ship That Voted No 7

Mutinies in the Royal Canadian Navy 11

The Vengeance of the Schooner *Nancy* 21

Christmas Eve Tragedy 25

RMS Titanic's Funeral City 33

Segwun 36

Picture Section 44

Canada's Last Liberty Ships — *Cape Breton* and *Cape Scott* . 48

The Fastest Ship in the World 52

The Hydrofoil *Bras d'Or* 55

The *Haida* in Winter 63

Canada's Last Carrier 72

The Corvettes 81

*In memory of my mother, Maifie,
who taught me to love the English language,
and my father, Jack, who taught me to do my duty.*

*And with thanks to my wife, Dianne,
for reasons she well understands.*

The Ship That Voted No

As the war in Europe approached its close, the Canadian government began making plans to be in on the kill against the Japanese. Canada had a substantial stake in the Pacific war: hundreds of prisoners taken when the Japanese overran Hong Kong. In addition, Canada wished to ensure her post-war status as a Pacific power, and did not wish the Americans to get all the glory.

Despite initial opposition from Washington, approval was finally given for an army division, an eight-squadron bomber force, and a fleet of two aircraft carriers, two cruisers and several frigates, destroyers and corvettes to take part in the action.

As it turned out, only one ship actually participated. The cruiser HMCS *Uganda* spent four months as part of the British task force operating north of the Philippines. Her most memorable part in this war was her manner of leaving it, a story so bizarre as to stretch credulity. But it really happened.

The Royal Navy cruiser *Uganda* was transferred to the Royal Canadian Navy at Charleston, South Carolina, on October 21, 1944. She had been laid down on July 20, 1939 by Vickers-Armstrong on the Tyne, launched August 7, 1941, and commissioned into the RN on January 3, 1943.

At 8,800 tons displacement, she was 555 feet long, 62 feet wide, and had a draft of 20 feet. Her four screws gave her a top speed just about 30 knots, and she could steam for 10,000 nautical miles at 12 knots. Her main armament comprised nine 6-inch guns, plus six 4-inchers, and ten 40-mm anti-aircraft mounts. Her crew numbered about 730.

Uganda, under Captain E.R. "Rollo" Mainguy, sailed in January, 1945, to join the British Pacific Fleet, linking up with Vice-Admiral Sir Bernard Rawling's force on April 8. For the next few weeks she helped screen the capital ships of the force, taking part in bombardments of remote islands and supporting air attacks against Okinawa.

But back at home trouble was brewing. The government had decided that all Canadian service in the Pacific would be voluntary, and all personnel now serving in that theatre had to be given a chance to volunteer anew. This decision was made public, and wives began writing to their husbands demanding that they come home and let those who had not yet done any fighting take their places.

When Rollo Mainguy received the signal asking if *Uganda's* crew agreed to volunteer to continue the war, the effect was staggering. The ship immediately became a seagoing debating society, with speeches for and against being made on all the messdecks. One wag christened the ship "The Snarling U."

About 75 per cent of the crew had fought in other ships, many in the Atlantic. Some were permanent navy; others volunteers who had signed up for the duration. They had not expected to be asked to do it again in this particular theatre.

Aboard *Uganda*, plans were made for a vote of sorts, giving the sailors a chance to sign a declaration as to whether they volunteered or not. Captain Mainguy was later reported in the press to have made the following statement:

"Anybody who signs that declaration is a quitter and I wouldn't want to be in his shoes for anything."

When those comments were published in a navy newspaper many years after the war, Mainguy's son, a retired vice-admiral, was moved to write a letter to the editor:

> Such a statement is so completely out of character with my father, that I do no believe it was made. My father quite understood the outrage of most of the ship's company at being asked to re-volunteer for service in the Pacific, at a time when they were already in the thick of the fighting there. I never heard him blame any member of the ship's company for exercising his vote against staying. My father felt betrayed by the political leadership which had interfered so directly with his own.

The fleet commander, Vice-Admiral Rawlings, kept a grim watch over developments aboard the Canadian cruiser. He messaged that he would not consider any reduction in *Uganda's* complement, which would impair her fighting strength and thus affect the safety of the British fleet.

On May 7, the vote was taken. Three hundred men voted to remain; 605 to go home.

The next day, May 8, 1945, word came that Germany had surrendered. But the Japanese fought on, sending in air attacks on May 9 that damaged two carriers. Captain Mainguy meanwhile signalled Ottawa that *Uganda* should stay on station until due for refit. But the government turned the idea down. Volunteer meant volunteer, and any man who didn't volunteer must come home. A bit of doggerel in the ship's newspaper summed it up, while also taking a swipe at Canada's diminutive and somewhat eccentric prime minister, William Lyon Mackenzie King:

I think I'll go home in the summer,
I think I'll go home in July,
Oh boy! I'll get fed
And I'll sleep in a bed
And I'll need no more love on the sly;
Come, let us sing
Of Ottawa's King -
Mackenzie's the name we adore;
The human torpedo,
As good as Bushido,
Uganda is out of the war.

But it didn't happen quite that quickly. *Uganda* stayed on station for several more weeks, causing increased discontent and bitterness below decks. On July 16 the British force joined Admiral Bull Halsey's U.S. fleet and sailed to within sight of the Japanese home islands.

As more British cruisers were coming out to join the fleet, and plans were also made for *Uganda's* sister HMCS *Ontario* to sail out to replace her, she turned for home. A British carrier signalled: "Goodbye . . . and good luck."

And so the Royal Canadian Navy's participation in the Second World War ended not with a bang, but a whimper. *Uganda* had voted herself out of the war, and she began the long voyage home. It was on August 7 she received word of the atomic bombing of Hiroshima — it was felt Japan would soon surrender.

It remained to a young Canadian fighter pilot, flying with the British Fleet Air Arm, to strike one final blow against the Rising Sun. Lieutenant Robert Hampton Gray, flying a Corsair off a British carrier, made a death-and-glory dive to sink a Japanese destroyer on August 9, posthumously winning the Victoria Cross, the Commonwealth and Empire's highest award for gallantry.

Uganda docked at Esquimalt, British Columbia, the next day, at a wharf crowded with reporters who had heard rumors of a mutiny. But it had not been a mutiny, it had been a vote, held with the encouragement of the Canadian government. Canada's war was over.

Postscript

After the war, *Uganda* was renamed HMCS *Quebec* and distinguished herself by becoming the first Canadian warship to sail around Cape Horn. She ended her days as a training cruiser on the East Coast, and was scrapped along with her sister ship *Ontario* in 1959.

Rollo Mainguy went on to a rewarding career both afloat and ashore. He is best remembered for heading the commission of inquiry into several small-scale mutinies in the RCN in the 40s and 50s.

Mutinies in the
Royal Canadian Navy

Mutiny. The word conjures up images from boyhood tales, of cutthroat pirates and high seas treachery. Ragged seadogs cheer as captain and mate are made to walk the plank. Retribution, when it comes, is a dangling noose from the yardarm.

But by the mid-twentieth century, mutiny was not that colorful or violent. The minor nature of these incidents in the Canadian fleet was out of all proportion to their effect on the future of a navy first formed in 1910, rooted in the Nelson tradition of the British senior service.

The mutinies, such as they were, mainly consisted of a refusal to work by crewmen aboard five different vessels in incidents spanning six years. The first two were quietly dealt with and then more or less forgotten. The latter three resulted in a report which shook the foundations of the service.

The first of these mutinies occurred during wartime, aboard the destroyer HMCS *Iroquois* in July 1943. An officer serving aboard her at the time later described it as "a locking of the lower fore mess doors." An inquiry was carried out by British naval officers, and their report to the Canadian authorities described as "a refusal of duty by a large section of the ship's company."

In 1947, there was a similar incident aboard the cruiser HMCS *Ontario*. It is significant to note that several ratings who were serving in *Iroquois* in 1943 were aboard the *Ontario* in 1947, and several crewman from the cruiser were likewise in the other three ships when their troubles broke out in 1949.

After the later three mutinies, the government ordered an inquiry. A board of commissioners, headed by Vice-Admiral E. Rollo Mainguy, conducted hearings and produced a report which, even today, strikes at the heart of what causes unrest aboard ships the world over.

One of the commissioners, Louis Audette, today remembers the sailors' complaints. After voracious reading on the subject of mutiny down through history, he has come to the conclusion that they all have the same root causes.

"The men aren't kept informed of what is going on," he says. "Then, their living conditions become intolerable or their officers behave intolerably. That last one was the big problem we heard about."

In fact, what caused the mutinies in the Royal Canadian Navy may well be described as "The Cruel Sea Syndrome" in that Canadian naval officers often adopted artificial English accents, took on exaggerated "old boy" mannerisms, and acted as if they were in an old British war movie.

In a news report published by the Canadian Press after the inquiry made its recommendations, a young sailor explained it this way: "Joe Blow and I come from the same town in Saskatchewan. We're below decks for a couple of years together. Then he gets to be an officer. Before you know it, I can't understand what he's saying."

There was a good reason for this, of course. When the first Canadian naval service was formed in 1910, it quite naturally depended heavily on the Royal Navy for expertise and ships. All through the First World War, Canadians served on British ships and vice versa, and this also occurred very frequently during the Second World War. In fact, secondment to the Royal Navy, known as "big ship time," was seen as an almost necessary part of a Canadian officer's career.

It was the occurrence of three separate mutinies in 1949, within weeks of one another, which finally spurred public action. Audette, in a published article written 30 years after the Mainguy Report, says the geography and sequence of these three occurrences are important to understanding them, given prevailing circumstances.

The mutiny aboard the destroyer *Athabaskan*, involving 90

men, took place at Manzanillo, Mexico, on 26 February. This was followed by a refusal to work by 83 crewmen in the destroyer *Crescent* on 15 March at Nanking. The third took place aboard the carrier *Magnificent*, under way in the Caribbean on 20 March. This involved 32 men, some of them aircraft handlers, of which more later.

All the mutineers were given full amnesty, plus a promise that their testimony would be kept secret. In fact, after the commission made its report to the then-minister of national defence, Brooke Claxton, Admiral Mainguy and commissioner Leonard Brockington destroyed their copies of the evidence. Audette, however, kept his for three decades. When everyone involved in the mutinies was finally out of the service, he donated 3,600 pages to the National Archives.

"The navy really didn't like the Mainguy Report," he says now. "The thinking chaps were pleased, of course, and nearly all of our recommendations were adopted later."

The Men Won't Come Up, Sir

Before we can deal with those recommendations, and what they meant to the navy of the day, it is necessary to have a further look at the mutinies themselves. The incident aboard *Iroquois*, occurring in wartime, was investigated by the Royal Navy. Very little information is available in files on the Mainguy inquiry, beyond the description quoted to Audette by the officer mentioned above. Audette himself, however, describes the cause of the incident as being her captain's "complete unsuitability for command."

The mutiny aboard the cruiser *Ontario*, however, is briefly described in the Mainguy Report, even though the commissioners were not looking into that particular incident.

Ontario was anchored off Nanoose Harbour, Vancouver Island, on 22 August, 1947, when several sailors requested an interview with the captain. The ship had been undergoing refit for two years, and this was her first short cruise since re-entering service.

Instead of seeing the men himself, the captain sent his executive officer. While on his way to see the men, the XO was met by the master-at-arms, who informed him that some of the sailors had locked themselves in one of the mess decks.

Now occurred one of the more interesting events which would be repeated in various ways throughout the other incidents and would even affect the inquiry. Because the penalties for mutiny were so severe, no one wanted to do anything that would make things worse. As a result, when the men in *Ontario* locked themselves in the mess deck, the captain did not order them out. In fact, no "Hands Fall In" pipe was made at all.

Instead the captain went to the public address system, and informed the entire ship that he was aware of the problem. He then said he would clear lower decks and talk to the whole crew in five minutes. He spoke to them for 15 minutes, and then everyone got back to work. Later, the captain studied the men's grievances, which are described in the Mainguy Report as dissatisfaction with "capricious" variation of the ship's routine, and with the executive officer. As a result, the officer was immediately transferred to another ship.

Here is how the commission of inquiry reacted:

> In retrospect, the speed of his transfer, without a complete investigation, appears neither completely wise nor completely fair. We examined the Executive Officer concerned at his request, and, having regard to the sense of injustice which he must have felt, he gave his evidence with highly commendable dignity, sportsmanship and objectivity. The incident involving the transfer of the Executive Officer was widely publicized ... throughout the Navy. We have already mentioned ... that men from the *Ontario* who took part in this incident, were subsequently drafted to *Athabaskan* and *Crescent*. The incident in *Athabaskan* was also known to the men in *Crescent* and *Magnificent*. It is, therefore, not surprising that in all four incidents, much of the alleged dissatisfaction was centred on ... the Executive Officer ... his removal was one of the major demands.

HMCS Magnificent

HMCS *Magnificent* was an aircraft carrier with a complement of 70 officers and 828 men, of whom 32 aircraft handlers were involved in the mutiny. On March 5th, 1949, she sailed from Halifax to Colon as part of Task Force 215, a joint Canadian-British formation.

On March 20th, she had been at "flying stations" almost continuously for three days. The flight deck crew had been awakened at 0500 that day, and a temporary halt due to weather was called an hour later. After all aircraft had been lashed down, the flight deck crew went to breakfast.

When the pipe to resume work was made, the chief petty officer found that only leading hands were present. He sent a petty officer below to find out what was wrong. The PO returned with the message that the men wouldn't come up. The CPO went below and found the 32 aircraft handlers sitting silently around a table. They did not speak, and he did not issue any orders. Again, this was likely because he was aware of the penalties for mutiny and did not want to provoke one.

Some time later the captain, along with the XO, came down and found the men engaged in routine cleaning of their mess deck. They stood respectfully when he entered, and he told them he would not tolerate any kind of mass grievance but would speak with them individually when time permitted.

When the next pipe to flying station was made, all hands obeyed. The captain later interviewed all the men involved, and no disciplinary action was taken.

Audette, in his article "The Lower Deck and the Mainguy Report of 1949," published in 1985, writes of the poor relationship between the XO and almost everyone else aboard, and how it led to the mutiny. "There were many cases of the injudicious assignment of men to tasks which more enlightened superiors would have been reluctant to assign them," he wrote. He tells of how aircraft handlers were assigned to clean up after officers' cocktail parties, and stewards were unforgivably deprived of shore leave to suit the convenience of certain officers.

"During a 'make-and-mend,' or afternoon off-duty, just before sailing for Britain, a number of aircraft handlers (the future mutineers) in HMCS *Magnificent* were detailed to secure automobiles brought on board by ship's officers. This assignment was so deeply resented in the circumstances, even by some of the officers, that it had to be cancelled before completion of the task, making the initial error even more apparent to everyone."

HMCS Athabaskan

The destroyer HMCS *Athabaskan* sailed from Esquimalt, on the British Columbia coast, on January 28th, 1949. She joined Task Group 215.9, commanded from the cruiser *Ontario*. Both captain and executive officer had only recently joined *Athabaskan* and were still feeling their way.

The destroyer was detached from the task group to go on ahead to Manzanillo, Mexico. She arrived there February 26th, and secured off the fuelling jetty. After lunch, the Chief Bos'n's Mate went topside to check on the crew of a whaler that was to be lowered away for a duty run, but there was no sign of the men. The duty petty officer went forward, and found the door to the crew quarters closed. When he tried to open it, he found that he could not, apparently because the men inside had dogged it down.

The duty PO shouted: "Come on, boys!" But there was no answer, and he returned to the Chief, who in turn reported to the coxswain and the Executive Officer. The captain was informed, and he went forward to the ammunition hatch, where the coxswain called down to the men to tell them that the skipper was there.

The men opened the door, and the captain entered and talked with them. He saw a piece of paper on a table which apparently had some demands written on it, but he covered it with his cap. A quick glance had showed him that it contained, among other things, a demand for the removal of the XO.

After returning from the mess deck, the captain ordered "Stand Easy" followed by a normal return to work. All hands reported for duty, and the ship left Manzanillo in mid-afternoon. Again, although some men were given cautions, no one was punished for the insubordination.

HMCS Crescent

On March 14th, the destroyer *Crescent* was in Nanking, China. When the British ship *Cossack* left that day, the captain of *Crescent* became the senior naval officer present, with responsibility for making and receiving a large number of social and diplomatic calls.

Just before leaving her home port of Esquimalt, *Crescent* had received a draft of 25 men from the cruiser *Ontario*, 15 of whom had been aboard her when the executive officer had been transferred as a result of the mass protest in 1947. The commission came to the conclusion that the incident aboard *Crescent* was planned the night before it happened.

On March 15th, "Hands Fall In" was piped after breakfast, but only senior hands appeared on deck. In all, 83 men had locked themselves in the mess deck, and they refused a subsequent pipe to clear lower decks. The captain, when he heard what was going on, assembled all the officers in his cabin, but they could shed no light on the matter.

Among the mutineers was an able seaman who was respected by all aboard. He was sent for, and the captain told him he wanted to speak to the men. In the meantime, someone had reached out and affixed a hand-written note to the outside of the door, which listed demands. These included the immediate replacement of the XO, the establishment of a welfare committee in accordance with navy orders, and a definite "Canadian" routine that would not be changed every few days. The note concluded, "Your first consideration is the ship's company, not your social functions ashore."

The able seaman escorted the captain down to the mess deck, where he spoke for several minutes. He told the men he was anxious to get to the bottom of their complaints, provided that they put them in individually in accordance with regulations.

After he left the mess, "Hands Fall In" was piped and everyone reported for duty. There were no further incidents, and no disciplinary action was taken.

"We are a Canadian Ship"

Notable among the hand-written demands posted on the mess deck door was the following:

"We are a Canadian ship and should have a Canadian routine."

The commission heard from many witnesses that there was a tendency aboard *Crescent* to follow Royal Navy routine in a manner which many thought slavish and unnecessary. There was also a feeling that the captain was devoting too much time to his social duties. However, both ship and captain were engaged on a mission unique in Canadian experience, isolated from other Canadian ships in rather bleak and inhospitable surroundings.

Audette says there was an almost universal opinion expressed at the hearings that the navy was not sufficiently Canadian. "In 1949, nothing distinguished Canadian ships or uniforms, and Canadian ships wore the white ensign of the RN as their national flag," he wrote in 1985. "The lower deck and a number of officers . . . resented this strange national anonymity of things."

Although there were "CANADA" flashes for the uniforms, most senior officers did not wear them, or want their men to wear them. One senior officer told the inquiry that he had never worn them in the past, and would not do so in the future, because it "spoiled" the uniform.

Another cause of unrest was the ships' welfare committees, or lack of them. They were supposed to provide sailors with a forum to discuss complaints, but in fact they either did not exist or seldom met. One executive officer told the inquiry that he disapproved of welfare committees and therefore had not formed one on his ship, even though naval orders required him to do so.

"In all three ships," Audette writes, "the men were aware of their officers' disobedience of orders on this score and resented having no forum in which to plead. It never seems to have occurred to the officers ... that their own defiance of orders led their men ineluctably down the path towards collective insubordination."

Audette also blames the artificial distance between officers and men for some of the trouble. This also included the false English accent and mannerisms adopted by some officers after their "big ship time" in the Royal Navy.

"It is still my opinion today that the survival of distinctions of speech and social class was inimical to the interests of the Royal Canadian Navy because they were foreign to Canadian usage and custom."

The Report

When the inquiry was over, the three commissioners submitted a report to Claxton containing several recommendations. Among them:

— In future, insubordination should be most severely punished;

— Immediate and thorough consideration should be given to a reform of the procedure governing the airing of general grievances and to the strengthening and widening of the organization of welfare committees.

The report also found that the incidents were technically mutinies, although there was no open defiance of a high officer's order, and no force was used. The inquiry also found there was no justification for the mutinous incidents or for any form of mass insubordination.

Audette, the only surviving commissioner, still has no doubts about what happened aboard those ships. The harsh penalties for mutiny led many people to refer to them as 'incidents,' and this style was also followed in the Mainguy Report.

"Thirty years later," Audette says, "I call them mutinies."

A Canadian Navy

The search for a Canadian identity went on and continues even to this day. Audette remembers when he was captain of HMCS

Coaticook, and one of his men was set upon and beaten by several American servicemen in Boston. The man was wearing a burberry overcoat with no markings, and when it was torn off during the fracas the "CANADA" flashes on his shoulders became obvious.

"They stopped hitting him and apologized," Audette remembers today. "They said they thought he was a British sailor."

No one involved in the Mainguy inquiry could have known that in less than 20 years, the Navy, along with the Royal Canadian Air Force and the Canadian Army, would lose its separate identity entirely, and be blended into the Canadian Armed Forces, in a common uniform. In 1967 Canadian sailors became the only ones in the world to wear green, and once again they began getting strange reactions in foreign ports.

Another two decades went by, and then in 1986 the newly-elected government of Prime Minister Brian Mulrooney restored distinctively-colored uniforms to the three services, and Canadian sailors once again ply the world's oceans in coats of navy blue.

The final word on this properly belongs to Audette, who now lives in Ottawa and continues his study of mutiny in history.

"The government of the day was desperately anxious when these things occurred," he says. "They were afraid of communist subversion, but we found no evidence of that."

Of the sailors who make up 90 per cent of a ship's company, he says: "If there is to be naval history, then it must be recognized that lower deck men stand side by side with admirals and officers in its making."

The Vengeance of the Schooner *Nancy*

Lieutenant Miller Worsley, Royal Navy, was in a tight spot, and he knew it. From his position on the shore of Nottawasaga Bay, looking out onto Lake Huron, he could see the sails of three warships approaching, and they were flying the Stars and Stripes of the infant republic to the south. It was August 13, 1814, and Great Britain had been at war with the United States for two years.

From the narrow spit of land on which he lay, the broad sweep of the Nottawasaga River curved behind Worsley, running almost parallel to the lakeshore. Stretching away to the horizon was a broad crescent of white sandy beach which to future generations would become a favourite resort area.

But now it was war, and the main cause of Worsley's concern sat quietly at anchor in the river behind him, her masts concealed by the trees. She was the schooner *Nancy*, and was his to command, along with 22 seamen, 23 Indians under another officer, and nine French-Canadian Voyageurs. This was Nottawasaga Landing, an important post on the British Supply routes, and guarded by a hastily-built blockhouse on the inland side of the river, overlooking the schooner anchorage.

The American ships sailed to the mouth of the river and dropped anchor, there to wait. They believed the British ship was still en route from Fort Michilimackinac. Perhaps *Nancy* would escape their eyes after all.

Nancy was built at Detroit in 1789, while that city was still British. Her construction was supervised by John Richardson of the Montreal firm of Forsyth, Richardson and Company. She was 80 feet long, 22 feet abeam, and her hold was eight feet deep. Richardson wrote to his partner:

> The schooner will be a perfect masterpiece of workmanship and beauty. The expense to us will be great, but there will be the satisfaction of her being strong and very

durable. Her floor timbers, keel, keelson, stem and lower futtocks are oak. The transom, sternpost, upper futtocks, top timbers, beams and knees are all red cedar. She will carry 350 barrels.

The *Nancy* was built for the fur trade, and carried food, rum, clothing, meat, powder and blankets up the lakes. She returned with furs, traded from the Indians. After her maiden voyage to Fort Erie in 1789 under Captain William Mills, John Richardson wrote: "She is spoken of here in such high strain of encomium as to beauty, stowage and sailing that she almost exceeds my expectations."

By 1812, she was still engaged in the fur trade, although under different owners, plying the waters of Lake Huron, Lake Erie and Lake Michigan. When the United States declared war, she was lying at Moy, now Windsor, across from Detroit, which had been ceded to the U.S. in 1796. She was immediately moved to Amherstburg, where she was commandeered as a naval transport by the local garrison commander. The British commander, General Sir Isaac Brock, received an inventory from his quartermaster which listed *Nancy* as capable of mounting six four-pounder carriage guns and six swivel guns.

Worsley had been warned that the Americans were coming by Lieutenant Robert Ramsay Livingston, a former Indian department courier. He had paddled across 300 miles of water to bring word from Michilimackinac Island. He had logged 9,000 miles by canoe in government service, and had so far been captured twice and escaped, and been wounded five times, losing the sight of one eye to a tomahawk.

While waiting for the American fleet to arrive, Worsley and his men hauled *Nancy* three miles upstream, under the lee of the blockhouse. Then the enemy sails came into view.

The attempt at concealment failed. An American wood-gathering party spotted *Nancy's* masts above the treetops, and a bombardment began. The Americans took howitzers ashore from their ships, and soon cannon balls and howitzer shells began to drop into the river and onto the ridge behind it. The American ships started landing the first of 300 assault troops; Worsley and Livingston knew they must act fast.

The American fleet consisted of the ships *Niagara*, *Tigress*, and *Scorpion*, under the command of Captain Arthur Sinclair, veteran of the Battle of Lake Erie the year before, in which the British fleet under Captain Robert Barclay had been defeated by Oliver Hazard Perry. Among them, they mounted a total of 24 guns against *Nancy's* three.

Worsley and Livingston prepared to withdraw, laying a powder train to blow up *Nancy*. Then one of the American shells crashed into the blockhouse, and *Nancy* burst into flame. Whether it was set off by debris from the blockhouse, or whether Worsley had time to light the fuse, is a matter for conjecture. But as the little party struggled inland away from the American bombardment, *Nancy* burned to the waterline and sank.

The Americans did not pursue. Instead the mouth of the river was blocked with felled trees, and the ships withdrew. Worsley, Livingston and their men emerged from the trees, uncovered a cache of food and supplies, and began a 360-mile paddle by canoe to Michilimackinac, quietly sneaking past *Scorpion* and *Tigress* which by this time were moored in Detour Passage, at the north end of Lake Huron.

When they arrived at the fort, they found the garrison on half-rations, as a result of the blockade. Worsley conferred with Captain Robert McDouall, the commander of the fort, and came up with a bold plan.

The following day, August 31, Worsley's force in four large cargo-boats, or bateaux, headed for the Detour Channel. The motley crew consisted of seamen from *Nancy*, members of the Newfoundland Fencibles Regiment, and Indians. Their mission was to capture the American ships, lift the blockade, and clear Lake Huron of the enemy.

On the night of September 3rd, after a reconnaissance by Worsley and Livingston, the four bateaux moved down upon the anchored *Tigress*, their oarlocks muffled. They were challenged, and the American ship opened fire, but by this time the British, Canadian and their Indian allies were swarming aboard. After a sharp fight, every American officer was wounded, including sailing master Stephen Champlin, a relative of Oliver Hazard Perry. Someone tried to burn the signal book, but Worsley seized it.

Livingston paddled off in a canoe to find *Scorpion*. He located her 15 miles away, beating up the channel towards *Tigress*. Worsley ordered the Stars and Stripes to be kept flying, and dressed his officers in American uniforms. *Scorpion* arrived after dark and anchored two miles away, unsuspecting.

At dawn, Worsley slipped *Tigress* and bore down on *Scorpion*, keeping his men hidden on deck, beneath their overcoats. There were no officers on deck aboard *Scorpion*, and the few crewmen scrubbing the deck paid no attention. *Tigress* closed to within ten yards.

A musket volley raked *Scorpion's* deck. Grappling irons were flung, and the fight was on. It lasted five minutes, and when it was over Sinclair's fleet was in British hands, and Lake Huron was secure. *Scorpion* was renamed *Confiance*, and *Tigress* was renamed *Surprise*. They ended the war under the Union Jack, and remained afloat until 1817 when the Rush-Bagot Treaty was signed, forbidding armed vessels on the Great Lakes. They were scuttled in Penetanguishene Harbour.

After the war, the British Admiralty awarded the North West Fur Company 2,200 pounds for the loss of *Nancy*.

The charred hulk of *Nancy* lay in the Nottawasaga River, and slowly the current carried tons of silt and sediment which built up, in and around her. Slowly an island was formed, and, almost a century after her sinking, in 1911, her hull was rediscovered by C.J.H. Snider. In 1924, an American 24-pounder shot was found on the river bank by Dr. F.J. Conboy, and the following year he located and dug up part of the hull. The federal and provincial governments became involved, as well as private citizens, and in 1928 the hull was raised and placed on display on the island. The present museum was built in 1968, and the ribs and keel are on display in a sealed building which also houses many artifacts and memorabilia of the period.

Christmas Eve Tragedy

Just under the surface of the North Atlantic, a few nautical miles outside Halifax harbour, the U-boat lurked in the half-light of the chill water, her periscope just breaking the waves. Above her, two-metre swells washed over the prismatic lens as the captain scanned the horizon for the tell-tale smudges of smoke that would indicate the presence of a convoy, outward bound with vital supplies for the Allied armies fighting in Europe against the increasingly-desperate forces of the Third Reich. The commander was wary, although this winter, five years after the start of the war, was not the Happy Time for German submarines that the first glorious months had been.

There were reasons for this, of course. Almost total Allied air superiority by now had virtually eliminated the surface attack, which was what the U-boat was actually designed for, being meant to use her submersibility as a means of approach and escape. And aircraft could even spot submerged U-boats, if the water was clear and not too rough.

There was slight chance U-806 would be spotted from the air this time, though. The sea was far too agitated, its surface roiled and heaving. No, the real threat was not human eyes, but ears, aided by a device first developed and named more than 20 years before, tagged with the acronym of the group which oversaw its development, the Allied Submarine Detection Investigation Committee — ASDIC.

Now, refined and more powerful, its eerie underwater ping had sounded the death-knell for many a brave Kriegsmarine U-boat crew. But there were ways to beat the ASDIC and still make a successful attack and escape. The commander of U-806 believed he had found one.

To the west, Convoy XB 139 was forming up outside Halifax harbour, its escorts taking station. Among them were two small vessels peculiar to the Royal Canadian Navy's role in this war. Aboard the Bangor-class minesweeper *Clayoquot* the crew were relaxed, enjoying the calm of the day before Christmas, and looking forward to the handing out of the special holiday "ditty bags" which the Navy League distributed to crews at this time of the year. Ship's writer Arthur Katz, now a private business accountant in London, Ontario, was 26 at the time, and in his berth amidships.

He says no one believed the Germans would be so ungracious as to do anything warlike on Christmas Eve.

"I mean that's the one day you figure it's going to be quiet," he says. "As a matter of fact, we had a cribbage contest in progress between the officers and men. At that point I believe I was still playing against the captain."

The "old man" on this run was Lieutenant-Commander Craig Campbell of Vancouver, and like all seven of *Clayoquot's* commanding officers, he was a reservist. Reserve officers were easily distinguished by the waved stripes of rank on their sleeves, and the reserve service, Royal Canadian Navy Reserve (RCNR) and the Royal Canadian Navy Volunteer Reserve (RCNVR) was known colloquially as the "wavy navy."

The Bangor minesweeper class carried one 12-pounder gun, one twin and two single Oerlikon 20-millimetre anti-aircraft cannon, and 40 depth charges. *Clayoquot*, like most of her sisters, had been ordered to leave her sweeping gear ashore and devote herself entirely to escort duties, on what came to be known as the Triangle Run — St. John's, Halifax, Boston and New York. She was 60 metres in length, displacing fewer than 700 metric tons. Her top speed was rated at 16 knots.

Today, four decades after the fact, that last figure still brings a smile to the face of Arthur Katz. "The ship would have to have been in tremendous condition to get that top speed," he says. "It was more like 12 knots."

Somewhere astern of *Clayoquot* and her 81-man crew was another member of the escort force, the corvette *Fennel*, commanded by Lieutenant-Commander Kenneth L. Johnson of Quebec City. She belonged to the famed Flower class, the little vessels which had a reputation for rolling in even the calmest water. Slightly larger than *Clayoquot*, she made about the same speed and had a crew of similar size.

As the convoy ploughed into the open sea, writer Katz remembers that not all the crew were being as punctilious about observing regulations as they might have been. "The rules were that you had to remain fully dressed at all times while at sea," he says, "even while sleeping. That way, if you had to go into the water, you had some protection from the cold. The regulations were that you never took your clothes off."

Katz was fully dressed, and was resting in his hammock. His life jacket was near at hand - in fact, he was lying on it. "We had a tremendous life jacket," he remembers. "It had pockets that contained just about everything you'd need to survive."

As the escorts took station with the convoy, Lieutenant-Commander Campbell assumed the role of convoy commander. Still, the realities of war did not seem too close at hand, for it was, after all, Christmas Eve.

"The ship was not at action stations, because we were just coming out of the harbour," Katz says. "Our cat-tails weren't even out."

And it was the absence of these cat-tails that spelled *Clayoquot's* doom, for these were a simple but effective counter-measure to the German acoustic torpedo, which homed in on the sound of the ship's screws.

The device consisted of two iron bars, separated by rubber spacers, which were towed, or streamed, behind the ship. They set up a clattering sound which one U-boat man described as "a power saw in labour" . . . causing the torpedo to veer astern of the target.

Now, as the convoy passed the Halifax buoy, U-806 began her stalk. The huge buoy, its bell sounding a sonorous peal across the waves, also reflected back from its submerged portion an ASDIC echo, which led the operators aboard to assume that it was the only thing they were hearing, when in fact the German submarine was getting set for the kill.

A few minutes after passing the buoy, all remained tranquil aboard the minesweeper. Ratings were at work beside depth charge rails on the stern deck, and several off-watch officers were resting in the wardroom. In *Clayoquot*, things were so cramped that one-third of the crew had to be "in the rack" at any one time, just to give the rest room enough to move about freely.

The slim metallic shaped lunged from the U-boat, its electric motor leaving no tell-tale wake of bubbles on the surface. It tracked onto the minesweeper's propeller, and detonated 250 kilograms of high explosive under her stern. The effect was cataclysmic.

The blast rolled up the after-deck like the lid of a sardine can, killing the ratings working there, and trapping the officers who were unlucky enough to be in the wardroom. Immediately after the torpedo struck, Arthur Katz looked astern from his office next to the radio room. He could see water pouring in through the after-deck. "It felt like we had hit a mine," he says. "There was a bang, a tremendous shudder . . . the ship came to a halt."

As the order to abandon ship came, Katz went over the side, down a line, into a Carley raft, which he describes as looking like "an oversize bagel." It capsized almost immediately, dumping him and several other crewmen into the frigid water.

When he tried to climb back onto the raft, he found that his fingers were too numb to enable him to grab on, and other hands reached down to pull him aboard. The men on the raft paddled frantically with their hands and with the oars provided to get away from the sloping side of their dying vessel.

"The captain just walked down the side of the ship," Katz remembers. "He was the last one to leave, he was real navy. Then he swam out to where the boats and rafts were."

As Katz and the others on the raft looked back at their sinking ship, they witnessed a horrific incident, one which stays vivid in his mind to this day.

> The officers that were down below . . . I'll tell you like it is. The ship at that time was aslant and we saw them sticking their heads out of the wardroom scuttles. Someone on the deck above released a Carley raft, and as it came down it struck one of them and broke his neck. Another pulled his head back as the water rushed in. That was a rough one . . . to see them die like that.

Now, from several hundred metres away, the chilled and agonized survivors watched *Clayoquot* die. Little by little, her stack dipped closer to the water.

"Finally she tilted," Katz remembers. "Then she just went straight down. I think the whole thing only took a couple of minutes. The worst part was watching the convoy steam away. They weren't waiting around to be sitting ducks for the submarine."

Then the men on the rafts caught sight of their enemy. A conning tower briefly broke the surface and slipped below a moment later. After the survivors were rescued, Sub-Lieutenant Victor Graves of Nelson, British Columbia, told reporters he believed he had also seen a periscope in the distance, under gunfire from a merchant ship.

But Katz puts little credence in the contemporary newspaper reports, vague as they were and subject to censorship. He smiles when he reads again how the men, chilled to the bone, were said to have been singing "Oh, Come All Ye Faithful" as they clung to the rafts.

"Believe me, there was no singing. We were all numb , in a sort of daze. You really can't believe that it happened that fast."

The men began the arduous task of pulling all the life-rafts together, no mean feat in the cold and heaving sea. But they were lucky, for about 45 minutes after the sinking, the corvette *Fennel* came pounding up and dropped her scramble nets to enable survivors to climb aboard. Her skipper ordered "All Stop" and put his ship's boat over the side as well. The corvette remained dead in the water for 12 minutes while the pick-up of survivors continued. *Clayoquot's* skipper was the last man out of the water.

The 73 exhausted survivor's were hustled below, to be stripped and rubbed down with coarse towels. Then they were put ashore at Halifax, described in newspaper stories of the day as "an eastern Canadian port."

Later, the captain of destroyers at Halifax, W.L. Puxley, paid tribute to Lieutenant-Commander Johnson and his crew for their efforts.

Katz and his shipmates spent Christmas Day, and several thereafter, in hospital. Then, issued new kit, they were sent on leave. "They treated us like heroes," Katz says. "You have to remember that was the Christmas rush, everyone was heading back to the main cities. But our crew had their own private sleeping car, and their own private dining car. They treated us very well."

Then, for Katz, came a bizarre denouement. Since joining *Clayoquot* in August, he had not told his wife, Yetta, that he had volunteered for sea duty. He had been employed in a clerical job in Halifax, but had asked for a ship in order to get abroad, and also to do something more meaningful in the war effort.

So while he had been in the North Atlantic, his wife had been receiving letters written ahead of time, and posted by her husband's friends from quiet, safe shore stations.

"I didn't want her to worry," Katz says. When he showed up unannounced at the front door in his ill-fitting survivor's uniform and told her that he had eight weeks' leave, her first question was: "Why, are you going overseas?"

"No," he said. "I've already been overseas."

Katz finished the war working in the discharge transit centre in Halifax. He had volunteered for service in the Far Eastern theatre, but to suggestions that he was a glutton for punishment, he says only, "I just wanted to see the world."

To this day, he maintains an active interest in naval affairs, and evinces great pride in Canada's naval force. He insists that, while officers make decisions, they don't run things.

"It was the chiefs that ran the ship, they were the ones who knew what to do. You can't trust officers to know that."

Now a grandfather, Katz says he will be grateful if none of his children or grandchildren ever has to serve in the military. He says war is a great waste of human life, but "If I had to go and fight for my country again, I'd do it. This is my country. But you keep hoping the necessity will never come about."

Katz says that despite the rigors of North Atlantic service and the horror of the sinking, one of the toughest tasks he ever faced came after he was safely back on land. Relatives of those lost visited the survivors in hospital, and Katz was asked if there was any chance that Sub-Lieutenant J. David Neil of Toronto was still alive, that he might have been taken prisoner.

With visions of the heads sticking out of the wardroom portholes passing before his eyes, he says: "That was one of the hardest things I ever did, to tell his mother to stop hoping."

The day after V-E Day, a lean grey shape eased into the harbour at Halifax past the silent watchful ships of the Royal Canadian Navy and the merchant marine. U-806, her hunting done, surrendered quietly. The newspaper stories about the surrender included the names of ships sunk by the marauder, and it was thus that Arthur Katz finally learned the precise identity and fate of his assailant. But he felt no enmity then, and feels none now.

"He didn't try to make it back or scuttle; he was a sensible man," Katz says of the submarine skipper. "He wasn't the kind of fanatic who would come out of the water and start shelling survivors. His job was to get the ship and that was that."

Then Katz pays his enemy the same compliment he addressed

to his own skipper, "This guy was a real navy man . . . The only grudge I held against him was that he was inconsiderate enough to sink us on Christmas Eve."

Arthur Katz kept in touch with one or two of his fellow survivors for a brief time after the war, but did not hear from any of them for years. He did hear that Lieutenant-Commander Campbell had dropped a wreath at sea, after the war.

It was up to his wife Yetta, now a comfortable and gracious grandmother, to keep clippings and several official RCN photos of the survivors. The one picture Katz had of his ship, he gave to his son.

But the pictures he keeps in his mind will be there for the rest of his life. For him, December 24, 1944, will never be forgotten.

"1944 definitely has to be my most memorable Christmas because how often is it you get another chance to keep on living?"

RMS *Titanic*'s Funeral City

For two weeks after the sinking of the Royal Mail Ship *Titanic* on April 15, 1912, bodies were being pulled from the chill waters off the North Atlantic. Some were hastily buried at sea, but more than 200 others were brought into the Canadian port of Halifax, Nova Scotia. Today, 150 graves in three cemeteries are still fastidiously maintained, reminders of a time that earned Halifax the name "The Funeral City."

Halifax is in one sense the birthplace of transatlantic shipping, for the city's best-known native son was Samuel Cunard. His shipping line shut down its offices in Halifax in the 1960s, but the big green and white tanks of the S. Cunard Oil and Gas Company still loom over the waterfront.

For hours on the 15th of April there was hope that at least some more survivors had been picked up by other ships. When it became obvious that *Carpathia* had them all, the ghastly truth began to dawn. More than 1,500 men, women and children were still out there in the North Atlantic. And because there had been no shortage of lifebelts, chances are hundreds of bodies were still floating.

Sightings of bodies had been made as soon as the sun rose that awful morning. Ships passing through the area reported their sightings when they arrived at Halifax, or they radioed them in. On Wednesday, April 17, White Star Line chartered the cableship *MacKay-Bennett*, which set out for the site of the sinking, 400 nautical miles south-east of Cape Race, Newfoundland. She carried on board 100 coffins, embalming fluid, and John Snow of Snow and Company, the area's leading undertaker.

For close to two weeks, *MacKay-Bennett* scoured the area, sending out boats to pick up the corpses bobbing in the swells. Hauling in the bodies, bloated and wearing the chest-girdling cork lifebelts, must have been a grisly chore. The *MacKay-Bennett* was joined in her labours by three other small vessels, the *Minia*, *Montmagny* and *Algerine*. One of the bodies recovered by the *Minia* was that of Charles M. Hays, president of the Canadian Grand Trunk Railway.

More than 100 bodies were deemed unfit to return to Halifax, and were buried at sea. The chief officiating clergyman was Rev. Canon Kenneth Hind of All Saints Cathedral, on board the *MacKay-Bennett*. On the *Minia*, services were conducted by Rev. Henry Cunningham, who brought back a souvenir in the form of a deck chair from the *Titanic*. This deck chair was donated to the Maritime Museum of the Atlantic by his grandson, David Waterbury, of Kentville, Nova Scotia. It now sits in a glass case, the five-pointed star on the backrest clearly visible.

The museum also has several other pieces of *Titanic* flotsam, including a cribbage board carved from a piece of wood by the *Minia's* carpenter, William Parker. There is also a section of oak trim panelling from above the forward entrance doors to the first class lounge, decorated with carved musical instruments. Two other pieces are a balustrade section and a newel post panel from the first-class forward staircase. This was the fabled "Grand Staircase" leading down from the passenger elevators.

It is likely this woodwork was smashed loose when the sea crashed through the skylight over the staircase. Or it may have been knocked apart by furniture tumbling past as the liner took her final plunge.

The smallest item on display is a brass button from an officer's uniform, bearing the pennant and five-point company star.

In all, 209 bodies were recovered. The class distinction that had served them as passengers also served them in death. Those who could be identified as first-class passengers were embalmed on board and placed in coffins before reaching port. The rest had to wait until they were ashore.

As the death-ships arrived, the pier was sealed off by a

contingent of special police brought in from Ottawa. Reporters were kept at a distance, but Jim Hickey of the Halifax Chronicle managed to cut a deal with Canon Hind. As the *MacKay-Bennett* steamed in, he went out in a hired tug and the minister dropped a list of names over the side. Hickey raced back to his paper and got a world-class scoop.

The bodies were taken off the ships and loaded into waiting horse-drawn hearses. They were taken to a make-shift morgue set up in the Mayflower Curling Club on Agricola Street, where certificates of death and burial permits were issued. Snow and Company brought in 40 embalmers from across the Maritime Provinces, and they set to work.

The millionaire John Jacob Astor was identified, not by the amount of money in his pockets, but by the embroidered "JJA" on his shirt collar. In the pockets of his blue serge suit the undertakers found 224 pounds sterling, $2,440 in U.S. currency, and five pounds in gold.

There was a dispute about the religion of some of the corpses. Four taken to the Jewish Cemetery, Baron de Hirsh, were found to be Roman Catholic. Fifty-five bodies were claimed by relatives; the rest were buried in numbered plots in three Halifax cemeteries, 121 in Fairview, ten in Baron de Hirsh, 19 in Mount Olivet.

And there they remain. Markers are simple, low stones with angled tops. Many bear no names, but read simply, "Died April 15, 1912."

Others are more eloquent. A larger stone on the grave of steward Ernest Edward Samuel Freeman reads in part:

"He remained at his post of duty, seeking to save others, regardless of his own life, and went down with the ship. Erected by Mr. J. Bruce Ismay to commemorate a long and faithful service."

Segwun

Early in October, the oldest working steam vessel in North America puffs her way across the deep dark lakes of central Ontario, her passengers bundled against the cold of the Thanksgiving weekend. They peer through binoculars and click cameras as the captain's voice over the public address systems tells them stories about the sumptuous cottages and summer retreats that line the shores and dot the islands.

Lunch is an elegant buffet at Windermere House, an historic resort hotel on the shore of Lake Rosseau. The passengers are ashore for two hours, long enough to stroll the grounds, admire the charm of the tiny town of Windermere, and make friends with the chipmunk that lives in a hole in the wall of the sun-drenched dining room. Then it's back aboard as the steamer chugs back to the lock at Port Carling, into Lake Muskoka, and then back to her home port at Gravenhurst. A full Ontario-style Thanksgiving dinner is served on the way, with turkey, sweet potatoes, and pumpkin pie topped with whipped cream. This is the end of the season, and the 102-year-old *Segwun* will now take a well-earned winter rest.

She is just a little steamship, a mere 128 feet long with a beam of less than 22 feet. Her twin double-expansion engines push her through the placid lake waters at a sedate nine knots. Yet this small Canadian passenger vessel is the last of a glorious and nostalgic fleet, the Royal Mail Ship *Segwun* of the Muskoka Lakes.

This year, this little green and white steamer is 108 years old, by far the oldest engine-driven ship in North America, and one of the oldest ships in the world still in commission.

"We're not running her to make a profit," says purser Nancy Kennedy. "The object is to keep her afloat and operating."

Afloat and operating. With three careers behind her, *Segwun* is now in her fourth, carrying tourists about the lakes she once plied as a vital link in the slower paced communication system of a bygone century. There were once more than 200 passenger steamers on the lakes of the Canadian province of Ontario, and their glory days lasted 130 years, from Lake Simcoe to Lake Abitibi, from Rainy River to the Rideau, from Muskoka to Madawaska.

She is one of the few remaining iron-hulled vessels left in the world. She now spends her days, lovingly restored, carrying passengers on dinner cruises, history cruises, and trips to see the summer homes of the rich and famous around the shores of the Muskoka lakes.

"Talking to people is what it's all about," says Captain James Caldwell. "That's why we have an open wheelhouse. I meet people every summer from all over the world."

Caldwell, a Great Lakes sailor for 29 years, shares his duties as captain with Tom Oake. They work three-and-a-half days per week, keeping *Segwun* on her full schedule of cruises. Caldwell delights in disconcerting his passengers by stepping from the wheelhouse as the ship leaves the dock, moving slowly in reverse for several minutes as the wheel stands untended.

"We're on rails," he tells the gaping tourists. "Just like at Disney World."

During the nineteenth century, steam power became a well-established source of transportation energy. In Ontario, then known as Upper Canada, steamboats and railways dominated the transportation business. Steamboats and trains were the only cheap, efficient and mechanized transportation to be had.

Canada's first steam vessel, *Accommodation*, was built in 1809 by John Molson to ply between Montreal and Quebec City. She was moderately successful, and was followed by *Swiftsure* and other steamers.

Steamboats steadily followed settlers and lumbermen inland, along the lake and river routes. Many communities were wholly dependent on the little lake steamers for communication with the outside world.

In 1886, on a night in early August, the side-wheeler *Nipissing* was docked at Port Cockburn, at the head of Lake Joseph, following her run from Gravenhurst. It was here that she had been launched in 1871, having been built at a cost of $20,000.

As she lay alongside in the quiet summer night, fire broke out in her engine room. The crew abandoned ship, and the steamer was cut loose to drift out into the lake. She grounded on Fraser Island, and burned to the waterline. Her skeleton lies there still, except for one of her ribs which is now in the Segwun Steamship Museum.

The smoke had hardly drifted away when the Muskoka and Nipissing Navigation Company began planning her replacement. The new steamer inherited the engine from the original ship, but *Nipissing II* was to have an iron hull, built in Scotland and shipped in sections across the Atlantic, then by rail to Gravenhurst.

She was commissioned in 1887, and served as the company flagship until 1902. Above her wheelhouse she bore a wooden phoenix, carved by commodore George Bailey, signifying her rise from the ashes of her predecessor. Passengers loved her for her paddlewheels and her soft, cooing whistle; officers liked her speed and manoeuvrability. Before the outbreak of the first World War, it was not uncommon for *Nipissing II* to carry more than 300 passengers and tons of freight on her voyages across the lakes.

She served throughout the first decade of this century and up to the beginning of the war, but her old power plant was beginning to give out. In the summer of 1914, the walking beam broke, and she had to be taken under tow by *RMS Islander*, one of her sister ships. Spare parts were hard to obtain, and the war years were lean ones for the company. So *Nipissing II* was tied up in Gravenhurst, and from time to time was used as a dormitory for employees.

Then came 1924, the middle of the Roaring Twenties, and prosperity was once more at hand. The ship's owners, now known as the Muskoka Lakes Navigation and Hotel Company, decided they needed a seventh steamer to add to the six already in service. So repair crews boarded *Nipissing II*, and stripped her of her old engine, pontoons and sidewheels. A new Scotch-marine boiler was rolled aboard, and twin screws were fitted, powered by two reciprocating, double-expansion engines manufactured at Goderich, Ontario.

The handsome new excursion steamer which was recommissioned in 1925 bore little resemblance to the old *Nipissing II*, so her owners gave her a new name, *Segwun*, an Ojibwa word meaning "Springtime."

Thus she embarked on her second career, under Capt. A.P. Larson of Gravenhurst, steaming between Bracebridge and Beaumaris, calling at Milford Bay, Port Keewaydin and Bala Bay, where she would meet the noon train.

Segwun was probably the fastest ship in the fleet, easily making around 18 knots. Her power-plant was set far enough aft to allow her to plane at speed. She sometimes would race the flagship *Sagamo* if they happened to be on the same course. But then the company had her drydocked, and fitted with new propellers, thus slowing her down. There were those who said this was done to avoid having *Segwun* outrun the flagship.

Her season usually began in early June, continuing until late September. In 1945, she was remodelled to include seven staterooms with toilets and double berths, and a bulkhead from the now-defunct *Medora* was installed at the forward end of the stoke-hold, to create crew sleeping accommodation. Next, in 1951, following the Noronic fire at Toronto, she was fitted with fire-fighting equipment.

By this time, *Segwun* and *Sagamo* were the only two steamships still in commission on the Muskoka lakes. Time was running out on an era, and in 1955 they were purchased by Gravenhurst Steamships, and operated for four more dwindling seasons.

Then, on August 5th, 1958, a junior helmsman, ignoring

instructions, took her onto a shoal and sheared off several propeller blades. Although her hull was undamaged, she limped back to Gravenhurst, her last trip. *Sagamo* continued to run until the end of the summer, and that was it until 1981.

Both ships remained tied up in Gravenhurst. *Sagamo* was converted into a floating restaurant, but was destroyed by fire in 1969. Her hull today is under landfill at Muskoka Wharf.

Segwun was saved by her owners, who sold her for one dollar to a group of citizens interested in preserving her. The town of Gravenhurst provided matching funds for those raised by the public, and the ship was cleaned up and filled with memorabilia of bygone days. As the Segwun Steamboat Museum, she was visited by thousands of tourists between 1962 and 1973.

However, as she sat alongside she began slowly to decay. Her hull was badly pitted, and her upper works began to leak and soften. There were many who were interested in seeing her restored to steaming condition, so that she would become a working museum, and pay her own way.

In 1969, marine engineer John Coulter arrived to fulfill a pledge he had made ten years earlier. He had served on the *Segwun* during his student days, and was determined to see her restored to operating condition.

The *Segwun* restoration project was born, and soon steam buffs and other interested people were coming forward. Tons of dirt and debris were removed from the bilges, and deckheads and sidewalls stripped of decades of paint. It was slow and frustrating work, and money trickled in.

By 1972 it seemed obvious that time was winning the race. Pinhole leaks were spreading in the hull, and the restoration committee turned in desperation to the provincial government. Although the government of Ontario promised $12,000 to help get the ship into drydock, salvation suddenly came from a completely unexpected quarter.

Several of the executives of the Ontario Road Builders' Association had cottages in the Muskoka district, and in March

1973 they invited the Segwun Committee to a special meeting at which they proposed that the association would sponsor a complete refit of the ship.

Funds and technical assistance would come mainly from the ORBA, which represents about 130 companies in the road construction business in Ontario. They would do this, they explained, as a public relations exercise, and to save a vessel of both historic and cultural significance. They also expressed a desire to make a form of atonement, as it was improved road communications that had helped put *Segwun* and others like her out of business.

A new group called the Muskoka Steamship and Historical Society was organized, and in August of 1973, *Segwun* was towed from her slip by *Lady Muskoka*, under Tom Oake, who would later come to *Segwun* as co-captain. She was fitted into the carriages of the marine railway, and gently hauled from the water.

Work could now begin in earnest, and the crumpled forepeak was the first piece of the hull to be cut away for restoration. Her hull was almost completely renovated, and two new bronze propellers fitted, replacing the old cast iron ones. Craftsmen under master carpenter Fred Kruger swarmed over the upper works, restoring the dining room and lounges.

On June 1, 1974, the prime minister of Canada, Pierre Trudeau, presided at the relaunching. Once towed back to her slip, *Segwun* was subjected to more work, as the entire hurricane deck and sections of the promenade deck were replaced with California redwood and British Columbia fir.

The engines were hauled out, inspected and rebedded, and new watertight bulkheads installed to bring her up to modern safety standards for carrying passengers. Modern generating equipment was installed, including solid state electrical panels, but no changes were made except those required for reasons of safety or compliance with modern regulations.

There were more problems to overcome, but slowly *Segwun* neared her moment of truth. On October 7th, 1980, she slipped from the pier and moved out under her own power for the first time in 22 years. Problems soon developed with the port engine, and she returned using only the starboard propeller. Nonetheless, repairs were made and the trials continued.

Then J. Ross Raymond, one of the Society's directors, came forward with a plan. He proposed reforming the old Muskoka Lakes Navigation and Hotel Company charter, and operating *Segwun* while at the same time raising funds. His idea was accepted, and in short order subscriptions came in, and the remaining engine work was completed. *Segwun* completed a shakedown cruise on June 21, 1981, and an official ribbon-cutting ceremony was held on June 27. It was time for her fourth career to begin.

Segwun today is a powerful tourist attraction to the Muskoka district, a region of lakes and cottage communities about two hours by road north of Toronto. She ran at a loss for the first five years, but in 1986 began to show a small profit. The Navigation Company has been merged with the society, and is optimistic about the future.

A mammoth century birthday party in 1987 saw a replica of the phoenix, carved by Bill Hunnisett of Guelph, once more placed atop the pilot house. Canada Post Corporation issued a commemorative stamp featuring a painting of the ship.

In her heyday, she carried 300 or more passengers. Today, she is licensed for only 99. With a crew of 12, she is expensive to operate. The coal for her fires comes from West Virginia, because of its low sulphur content and low ash formation. The ash is also slightly alkaline, and it is shot into the lake using an "ash gun" powered by her own steam.

"The lake is slightly acidic, so if we are doing anything to the environment we are helping it," says engineer Rob Allen, who has a background in marine engineering and has served on the Great Lakes. "That's why we use the West Virginia coal, because of concerns about pollution."

Purser Nancy Kennedy oversees a dining room that will seat

32 people. It is used for dinner and luncheon cruises, as well as afternoon tea. "Everyone comes aboard to have a good time, and it creates a pleasant working atmosphere," she says. "They are even more surprised when they have a good meal."

Weddings are often held on board, and private charters are increasing. Recently, when a daughter of the Culotta winemaking family was married aboard, the winery blended a special bottling under the ship's own label, and this is now served in the dining room. It can also be purchased in the Gravenhurst liquor store, and is a favourite with visitors.

The crew are also well-versed in the ship's history, and Capt. Caldwell likes to point out the rings fitted into the sidewalls on the main deck.

"Lady Eaton used to bring her horses up here in the 30s," he explains. "They tied them up to these."

Cruises ranged from 90-minute family outings, to overnight escapes to a lakeside resort. Prices range from $9.00 single adult fare to $175 for the two-day getaway. Many of the cruises feature dinners and buffets, and stops at local resorts and plush cottages owned by wealthy old families.

Although the fares cover the cost of operating the ship, there is still the constant work of keeping her in shape. For this reason, a group calling itself "Friends of the *Segwun*" solicits donations to help pay for periodic drydocking and any major repairs. Because the operation of the ship is non-profit, these donations are tax-deductible.

Specialty cruises are run each season, as well as regular runs. Further information can be obtained by writing to:

The Muskoka Lakes Navigation and Hotel Company Limited
Box 68, Gravenhurst, Ontario CANADA P0C 1G0

Picture Section

All photos courtesy the Maritime Command Museum

The hydrofoil *Bras d'Or* at speed. Taken during trials in the Halifax approaches July 1969.

The last corvette, HMCS *Sackville*.

HMCS *Uganda* sailing around Cape Horn.

HMCS *Clayoquot*.

The survivors of HMCS *Clayoquot* in the water, about to be picked up. The commanding officer is at lower left, looking up towards the camera.

HMCS *Niobe*, which along with HMCS *Rainbow*, formed the first Canadian naval service in 1910.

All gone now. Two Banshees, a Tracker, and HMCS *Bonaventure*.

Canada's Last Liberty Ships — *Cape Breton* and *Cape Scott*

She is the last of ten Liberty-ship type vessels built in Canada in 1945, just as the war in Europe was coming to a close. Today she sits, still afloat, in the naval harbour at Esquimalt, British Columbia, across the Strait of Juan de Fuca from the Burrard Drydock where she was laid down almost half a century ago.

Cape Breton was until 1994 still a working unit of the Canadian fleet, even if she was no longer really a ship, technically speaking. Her hull and superstructure housed Fleet Maintenance Group (Pacific), 123 officers and ratings.

FMG(P) provides a variety of marine and combat systems repair to the ships of Canada's Pacific squadrons. The unit moved ashore into a new building in 1994, and *Cape Breton* will never steam again.

Cape Breton and her sister ship, *Cape Scott*, were commissioned into the Royal Navy in 1945 as escort maintenance ships. The *Scott* served first in the Far East, as *HMS Beachy Head*. Later, she was transferred to the Dutch navy, as HNMLS *Vulcaan*.

After service in the Far East with the Dutch navy, she was returned to Canada by the Royal Navy in 1951, and renamed *Cape Scott*. After conversion to a mobile repair ship, she was commissioned in the Royal Canadian Navy at Halifax in 1959. But it was in November of 1964 that she began her greatest adventure, under the command of Charles Anthony "Tony" Law, who later became a well-known artist.

"It was my last command, and I planned the trip myself," he remembers. "McGill University (in Montreal) had sponsored a 42-member expedition to Easter Island, and eight of them were women. This was the first time the Royal Canadian Navy had taken women to sea."

Cape Scott carried aboard a solar water distillation plant that had been designed at McGill. It was to be installed to provide the islanders with a reliable source of fresh water.

"We ran into one God-awful storm during the night, so I headed straight for Africa," Law recalls. "Then the next day I was able to alter for Bermuda, San Juan and the Panama Canal."

At the canal, the pilot came on board in wide-eyed wonder. "Don't tell me she's a Liberty ship!" Commander Law replied that yes, it was a Liberty ship.

"She does eleven knots, and if the laundry's running its ten-and-a-half. If I run into any wind at all she doesn't go anywhere!"

Commander Law used the chart for Easter Island which had been surveyed by Captain James Cook in 1770. "I anchored where he suggested."

The regular Chilean supply ship had for some reason failed to turn up at the island, and the residents were getting perilously short of vital supplies. The governor asked Commander Law for help, and the crew of *Cape Scott* turned to provide food from the ship's stores. A camp was set up ashore, and the doctors and scientists from seven countries on the university team began a survey of the Polynesian families on the island.

The ship's canteen was opened to sell soap, toothpaste, and other sundries, and soon the governor was calling again on Commander Law, this time with a different problem.

"We had ended up with all the money on the island, so he couldn't operate the government. I had to give him some of it back, in return for a receipt."

On the return journey, *Cape Scott* carried youngsters from Easter Island who were going to school in Valparaiso. They celebrated Christmas in mid-ocean, with a tree from Nova Scotia. The next two months were spent visiting the Chilean navy in various ports along the mainland coast.

Cape Scott was still at sea when the new Canadian flag was proclaimed. Scrounging some red and white bunting from the Chileans, Law's crew stitched up their own rough-and-ready version of the red maple leaf, and held a solemn ceremony.

Cape Scott arrived back in Halifax in March of 1965. She continued to serve out of that port until 1970, when she was paid off into reserve. She resumed active life briefly two years later by becoming Fleet Maintenance Group (Atlantic), but the organization moved ashore in 1975. *Cape Scott* began her last voyage in 1978, under tow to be scrapped in Texas.

Her sister ship, *Cape Breton*, was originally commissioned in the Royal Navy as HMS *Flamborough Head*. Under terms of an agreement between Britain and Canada, it was decided that these ships would be retained on loan by the RN for as long as required, and then they would be returned to Canada. When the offer was made to return *Flamborough Head* in 1950, the Korean War had broken out, and the Canadian navy had begun an expansion program. She was therefore formally accepted into the RCN in May 1951.

She was at first employed as a floating naval trades school, to train young men to petty officer level in various technical services. Fitted with classrooms, work-shops and living space, she was renamed HMCS *Cape Breton* under Commander E.N. Clarke, the first engineer officer to ever skipper a Canadian naval vessel. Sixty-six seaman apprentices were on board to begin their two-year training courses in such trades as engineering artificer, shipwright, electrical technician, air artificer and armorer.

Cape Breton continued in her role as a floating schoolhouse for five years, alongside the jetty in Halifax. Then the apprentice school was moved ashore, and *Cape Breton* sailed from Halifax on August 25, 1958, for the west coast anchorage at Esquimalt. There she was paid off for conversion to a mobile ship repair, later designated an escort maintenance ship.

When the refit was completed, *Cape Breton* was equipped with engineering and electrical workshops, a blacksmith shop, and a plate shop. Manned largely by technical personnel, she was capable of providing all manner of electrical and diesel engine service, electronics repair and communications maintenance, as well as hull repair. Her helicopter landing platform allowed the replenishment of stores and equipment by air.

She spent a lot of time alongside in Esquimalt, tending to the needs of the fleet there. But she also sailed with the ships, ranging as far as Pearl Harbour.

In 1964, *Cape Breton* was again paid off into reserve. But in 1972, she was resurrected once more, and became Fleet Maintenance Group (Pacific), a towed mobile support unit and accommodation vessel. Now she awaits her fate.

The Fastest Ship in the World

She was the fastest ship in all the world, and her name was *Marco Polo*.

In 1850, the world was six months around. It was accepted as fact that no sailing ship would ever do it in less. It took 100 to 120 days to reach Australia from England, even in the fastest clippers.

In 1851, however, shipbuilder James Smith of Saint John, New Brunswick, was putting the finishing touches to a vessel that would show the world what speed really was. She would be a leader, and would become a legend.

It was one of the largest hulls ever built in a Canadian yard, a unique design combining the underwater shape of a clipper, with the midships girth of a cargo carrier. Framed of tamarack and pitch pine, she was planked with oak and pine.

Then came her launching on April 17, and the mishap that may have contributed to her speed. As *Marco Polo* slipped into the water of Marsh Creek, she ran away from her line handlers, and beached herself firmly in the mud. It took two days to set her free, and it was then discovered that the grounding had caused her keel to hog in the centre, leaving it six inches higher amidships than at bow and stern.

She showed her speed on her maiden voyage, charging across the Atlantic to Liverpool under the command of Captain William Thomas of New Brunswick. Laden with timber, she made the passage in just 15 days. On future voyages she carried cotton from Mobile, and one of her skippers, Captain Amos Crosby of Yarmouth, Nova Scotia was so taken with her that he commissioned a painting.

Then in 1852, gold was discovered in Australia. *Marco Polo* joined the Black Ball Line of Australian Packets, and new owner James Baines had her refitted as a luxurious passenger ship, capable of carrying a thousand souls amid maple panelling, crimson velvet upholstery, stained glass doors and circular glass hatchlights.

On July 4, 1852 Captain James Nicol "Bully" Forbes of Aberdeen took the great ship to sea, pointing her towards the Southern Ocean. Bound for Melbourne with 930 passengers and 60 crew, *Marco Polo* stood out in the Atlantic and then she flew. Flying before the gale winds that blew from the west day after day, she entered Melbourne just 76 days later, whereas before 100 days had been considered a smart passage. In four days alone, she had covered 1,344 miles; 364 miles being her best day's run.

She left Melbourne for the return journey on October 11, 1852, passing south of New Zealand to Cape Horn, then up across the Equator to the Irish Sea and back to Liverpool. Again, only 76 days passed from berth to berth, and *Marco Polo* returned to England after circumnavigating the world in five months and 21 days, including 17 days in Australia. As she sailed up the River Mersey, a banner between her masts proclaimed "Fastest Ship in the World."

Over the next 15 years she reigned supreme, no other ship could touch her speed. In 1867, despite the ravages of time and hard sailing, she completed her last passage from Melbourne to Liverpool in just 76 days.

As the years passed, she reverted to her first calling, carrying cargo along the trade routes of the world. By the early 1880s, she had become a tramper, carrying everything from timber to coal to guano. In July of 1883, she sailed from the Quebec shore of the St. Lawrence with a load of timber for Europe. Her hull by now was so weakened that it was bound about with chains, and her pumps worked round-the-clock to hold the leaks at bay. By July 25, she was off Cavendish, Prince Edward Island, and caught in the grip of a summer gale. The pumps could no longer keep up, and one of the chains snapped. Her captain, commanding a crew of Norwegians, Spaniards, Swedes, Tahitians and one German, decided the only way to save his men and cargo was to beach *Marco Polo* on the sandy shore of the island.

A young girl standing on the beach vividly remembered the

great ship, driving towards the shore "coming before the gale, with every stitch of canvas set — a sight never to be forgotten!"

Marco Polo struck about 300 yards out, and the crew immediately cut away the rigging. The great foremast and the iron main-mast went over with a roar and crash that could be heard clearly above the howling of the wind. The crew prepared to take to the boats, but the people on shore, aware of how deadly the surf was, held up a hand-lettered sign: "Stick to the ship at all hazards!"

Marco Polo had by this time broached to, and the waves were breaking over her. But she held together through the night, and in the morning a boat put out from shore and rescued the entire crew.

Some of the cargo of deal planking was salvaged in the ensuing weeks, but tragedy, which had so far stayed its hand, was to make one final play. About a month after the grounding, three of the salvors decided to spend the night on board the wreck. A storm came up, and they were stranded. A crowd gathered on the beach as the men attempted to launch a boat. They were thrown into the raging surf, and one of them, Peter Buote, was swept away and his body not recovered for some days. The other two scrambled back aboard *Marco Polo*, and clung there desperately as the ship began to break up.

The young girl who had witnessed the grounding was there.

"At last, towards evening, the sea grew a little smoother. And, though the attempt was still fraught with danger . . . a party of brave men went to the rescue. They reached the wreck in safety and hauled the men on board by means of ropes. Thus they were all brought safely to land, exhausted with cold, wet and hunger, but still alive."

It took another week for the last signs of the great ship to disappear. The girl who had been a witness to the drama wrote an essay about it for a contest in the Montreal Witness, and won first prize. This inspired Lucy Maud Montgomery to a great calling, and she would soon become famous as the author of "Anne of Green Gables," the novel that has since become the basis for a large part of Prince Edward Island's tourist wealth.

The Hydrofoil *Bras d'Or*

She made 66 knots, could turn on a dime, and was the latest concept in anti-submarine warfare. But in the end, she fell victim to short-sightedness, and the country that gave her birth finally had to admit that it had become just another customer of foreign technology.

She was named *Bras d'Or*, after the lake in Nova Scotia on which Alexander Graham Bell had first conducted his hydrofoil experiments. A subtle melding of aviation and marine technology, she ended her days as a museum exhibit.

But briefly, this slender craft caught the imagination of thousands, and became for many then serving the final achievement of the old Royal Canadian Navy, in the last moments before all three services were blended into a common green uniform.

Her story began in the quiet lake district of Nova Scotia, where an expatriate Scottish genius named Alexander Graham Bell conceived that a water-craft might far exceed known speed and performance limits by being able to rise above the water on stilts, and plane along on thin strips of metal or wood. Bell and Frederick Walker Baldwin began to experiment with ladder-like hydrocurve surfaces, and in 1918 developed the HD-4. One year later, with new engines, this craft set a world speed record of 70.86 miles per hour, a record for hydrofoil craft which stood until well into the 1950s.

When war broke out in 1939, Baldwin worked with the Royal Canadian Navy and the United States Navy to develop lightweight hydrofoil targets. When it was found that aircraft trying to lay smoke were highly vulnerable to ack-ack fire, Baldwin designed a hydrofoil with a two-man crew that performed exceptionally well in trials. This led to production of the radio-controlled "Comox Torpedo" smoke-layer.

After the war, Lieutenant-Commander Duncan Hodgson, a reserve naval officer who had worked on the Comox Torpedo project, was recalled to full-time service to work with the Defence Research Board on developing a hydrofoil craft. A design was submitted in 1948, and this became R-100, a craft later named *Massawippi*, after the lake in Quebec where she was built. R-100 was completed in 1950, and taken by train to Halifax for trials. She was 45 feet long, eight-and-a-half feet abeam, and was powered by a Packard-Merlin aeroengine developing 1,250 brake horsepower and 3,000 revolutions.

On July 13, 1950, despite teething problems, R-100 hit 64.28 knots at 2800 rpm. Various changes were made to the foils as testing continued into 1952. At the same time, planning and designing of advanced prototypes continued, and in 1957 a teardrop-shaped vessel designated R-103 was launched at Saunders-Roe on the Isle of Anglesey. Named *Bras d'Or*, she proved unstable in initial trials, and fell off her foils at 25 knots, doing extensive damage. It was decided to move her to Canadian waters for further testing, and she was loaded aboard the new RCN aircraft carrier, *Bonaventure*, which had been built at Harland and Wolff Shipyards. The "Bonnie" and her precious cargo arrived in Halifax on June 26.

Full-scale testing began the following spring on a measured course in Bedford Basin. Later, this craft was renamed *Baddeck*, and was used as a high-speed tug in the development of the variable-depth sonar still used by the Canadian navy today. Other prototypes were developed over the next decade, including *Proteus*, derived from "Propulsion Research and Ocean-Water Testing of Experimental Underwater Systems."

But it was the Royal Canadian Navy's objective to produce an operational vessel, a winged anti-submarine warrior capable of patrolling the North Atlantic sea lanes. This project, designated FHE-400, resulted in a three-phase contract being signed by DeHavilland Aircraft of Canada in 1963, calling for final sea trials and the handing over of the ship to the Royal Canadian Navy by

1969, when it was felt that firm proposals would have to be made to replace the old steam frigates then in service.

The hull was built upside down on a special jig by Marine Industries Limited of Sorel, Quebec, then rolled upright after completion. The superstructure was then lowered into place and welded on. The foilborne propulsion system was developed by Canadian General Electric, on behalf of its parent company General Electric of Lynn, Massachusetts. The American firm had previous experience with hydrofoils in the USN, notably the Denison and AG(EH) Plainview programs.

FHE-400, to be named *Bras d'Or* now that the earlier prototype had been renamed, was fitted with fixed-pitch, three bladed super-cavitating propellers jointly developed by DeHavilland and the ship division of the National Physical Laboratory in Great Britain. They were actually built by the Ladish company of Milwaukee.

The engine to power the craft when foil-borne was the FT4A-2, a derivative of the J-75, produced by United Aircraft of Canada. It delivered 25,500 horsepower and 21,500 revolutions under normal operation. The engine was mounted on the upper deck, abaft the pilothouse, and coupled to the CGE-built transmission through 30-foot shafts down through the hull and out into the foils.

For hullborne power, she was fitted with a Davey Paxman Ventura diesel driving two controlled pitch propellers built by KMW of Sweden. Mounted 30 feet apart, they provided great manoeuvrability at low speeds, and in confined waters. Auxiliary power was provided by a ST6A-53 gas turbine, which was also capable of boosting the diesel engine in a combined drive arrangement. In the event of engine failure, it could drive the vessel at low speed.

There was also a fourth engine, a GTCP85-291 emergency turbine, which could supply essential power in an emergency via a generator and seawater pump for firefighting. All four engines used a common fuel, normally JP5, but could run on JP4 or marine distillate if necessary.

As for accommodations, *Bras d'Or* was not wanting. An ultramodern galley and crew spaces were designed by Timmins Aviation, to include microwave ovens, freezers, and electric pans. Bunks were athwartships, instead of fore and aft, and storage space for personal kit was extremely tight.

But this new *Bras d'Or* was intended to be not just a prototype but a fighting ship, and plans were developed to fit her with a complete combat suite, including triple launchers for Mark 36 torpedos, a computer-controlled information centre to provide firing solutions and update the tactical picture for sonar and radar operators, along with AN/SQS 507 sonar, Phillips radar and AIS Hughes display equipment purchased from the United States Navy. However, not all of this was accomplished during the vessel's lifetime.

Disaster struck the project on November 5, 1966. That afternoon, a test team from deHavilland was putting the electrical generating system through its paces, when a hydraulic leak developed. The fluid sprayed onto the hot exhaust stack, and ignited, filling the immediate area with flame and acrid smoke. One technician was badly burned, and the blaze soon raced through the hull. Four firemen from the shipyard arrived and began to battle the blaze, and the Sorel fire department was called. The fire was put out about 90 minutes after it began.

Damage was extensive, with the deck and hull burned through in places and buckled in others. Interior machinery was ruined. It looked as if the project might even be cancelled. But the government, after four months of investigation, decided to continue. The contract was re-negotiated, and a joint management review committee was formed to oversee the whole project. DeHavilland and MIL began removing the fire-damaged machinery, and work was begun to rebuild the hull.

But by this time it was obvious that *Bras d'Or* would not make it into the water in time to be thoroughly tested as a replacement type by 1969, when the navy's new equipment procurement program was due to be made final. The fire had robbed her of any chance of becoming the next generation of Canadian warship. It is considered almost universally that it takes ten to eleven years for a new weapon or ship type to be developed. The Bras D'Or program had tried to do it in five-and-a-half, and had almost made it.

In July 1968 *Bras d'Or* made her way, in a slave dock, under tow to Halifax. On the 18th, a bottle of champagne was broken across her forward foils. Commissioned into the Royal Canadian Navy, she became Her Majesty's Canadian Ship *Bras d'Or*, just as the RCN itself was yielding to the government's plan for a single unified fighting force. On July 23, the slave dock was submerged beneath her, and *Bras d'Or* floated free for the first time.

Alongside testing, with numerous system failures and glitches, went on throughout the rest of 1968 and into early 1969. It was not until April 9 that her captain, Commander Constantine "Tino" Cotaras judged her ready to become foilborne. Seated at the controls in the cockpit-like bridge, Cotaras and helmsman Chief Petty Officer Barry Howles slowly brought the revs on the turbine up to and beyond 2,000. At 2,500 rpm, *Bras d'Or* popped up on her foils and tore off downrange, hitting 35 knots and leaving a mist of smoke and spray behind her. She could fly!

In July she was weighted down to simulate the load of her fighting equipment. During this period she exceeded her design speed of 60 knots, hitting 62 knots on July 9th. By 1970, numerous glitches had been ironed out, although many problems remained, and it was at this time that a new commander, Gordon L. Edwards, arrived on the scene. The Royal Canadian Navy was no more, having been merged into the unified and common-green Canadian Armed Forces, and *Bras d'Or* was being seen increasingly as a problem-plagued lame duck, always having to be towed back into port.

Edwards took an upbeat approach, even though rumors were flying that the government was thinking about canning the project. The former carrier fighter pilot and jet instructor, who had served on exchange duty aboard USS *Independence* and USS *Intrepid*, decided then and there that never again would FHE-400 be towed into harbor. He proved this later in the year by using the auxiliary systems to power his way home when the main drive system quit.

Edwards and his crew conducted the first overnight cruise on *Bras d'Or*, finding that the small hydrofoil was surprisingly steady even in a quartering sea. However, it was noisy inside the hull, and there were only 28 bunks for 37 personnel, as 15 civilian workers were also on board. Living aboard was spartan, to say the least. Longer exercises were conducted with other ships, and it was found that *Bras d'Or* could dance around them in 15-to-20 foot swells, making figure eights in order not to outstrip them as they ploughed on through the waves.

In May, 1971, Edwards showed off his little ship to the fleet in Bedford Basin. He describes the scene in Thomas G. Lynch's book, *The Flying 400*:

> I overdid it a little. After doing a slalom down the formation . . . I gilded the lily by going past the flagship literally waggling my wings. I was accordingly told by Commodore Willy Hayes, 'That will be quite enough.' Any naval officer can quickly grasp the significance of the adjective 'quite' and so I quickly left the Bedford Basin.

It was then time for an ambitious project. Edwards planned to take his tiny ship and her crew 2,500 miles to Bermuda, unescorted. From there she would go on to Norfolk, Virginia, and thence back to Halifax. Several exercises and demonstrations were also planned to take place during the trip.

At Hamilton, Bermuda, *Bras d'Or* arrived foilborne and then settled gently onto her hull in front of the Princess Hotel. Thousands of local residents and tourists toured the ship during her stay, and on June 21st the governor of Bermuda came aboard for a demonstration run. Immediately after dropping the governor and a group of reporters, *Bras d'Or* refuelled and headed for

Norfolk, meeting the USS *Marblehead* en route. Edwards performed a couple of figure-eights around the American ship, beeped his horn like the road-runner cartoon character, and then took off for the horizon in a shower of spray.

She entered Hampton Roads on June 23, making a pass at Pier Seven and then berthing stern first. Briefings and demonstrations were then carried out over the next few days for high-ranking USN officers and foreign visitors.

There were more problems, of course, but *Bras d'Or* made it home to Halifax in fine style on the 29th. Bands played and flags waved as the little ship entered into the harbor on her foils and settled gently into her berth. Edwards and his crew had proved that the hydrofoil could cover long distance in heavy seas on her own, repairing her own breakdowns as she went.

In August Edwards was posted to the NATO Defence College in Rome, and no replacement was named. Uncertainty clouded the testing program as the summer wore into Autumn, and then on November 2nd, the minister of national defence, Donald MacDonald, told the House of Commons that the project was to be scrapped. Because there was little chance of off-shore sales, and because the Canadian navy was switching emphasis from anti-submarine to sovereignty protection, the hydrofoil wasn't needed. The official announcement said *Bras d'Or* would be laid up for five years, but realists knew the whole program was dead, and she would never sail again.

By the new year, the remaining crew were engaged in preparing the ship for storage. On May 1st, a sombre de-commissioning ceremony was held, and *Bras d'Or* was towed on a slave barge to a remote corner of the Halifax dockyard to await her final fate. By 1976, it was obvious that five years really meant "forever" and the petty destruction began. Her spare parts were sold off, and the super-cavitating propellers were turned into scrap. As the years passed, the bunks, radios, diesels, and other interior gear were stripped out. By 1982 she was little more than an empty shell. Author Thomas Lynch visited her and described the interior as running red with hydraulic fluid, like the bloody carcass of a slaughtered animal.

As those trying to save at least something of the ship were beginning to admit defeat, a little-known museum entered from the wings. The Bernier Museum of L'Islet-sur-Mer, Quebec, said it would like to keep and display the craft, and negotiations began. By summer a deal had been struck, and on June 6th, the tug *Techno Venture* towed *Bras d'Or*, atop a slave barge, out of Halifax for the last time. She is now firmly fixed ashore, and on public view.

The real tragedy of the *Bras d'Or*, however, like that of the Avro Arrow, was the loss of confidence, and the "brain drain" of innovative engineering and design teams who immediately fled south in disgust and despair.

The *Bras d'Or*, like the Arrow, was a miracle of jet-age achievement. Although she was an experimental craft, she carried a lot of hopes and dreams with her as she raced about on her foils. Those hopes and dreams also went into drydock in 1971, never to return.

Haida in Winter

She has spent a good deal of her life in winter, and accomplished many of her greatest exploits in howling winds and frigid seas. Now, she lies moored in an inland sea of fresh water, and when winter comes, she is coddled in ice-breaking bubbles, her tender extremities covered with green plastic bags. Only one person moves about her decks these long months, retired navy skipper Bob Willson, answering the phone, planning tours by Sea Cadets and school groups, and remembering life aboard this great fighting ship.

"She was a good ship, and we had a good wardroom in those days," Commander Willson remembers of his service aboard Her Majesty's Canadian Ship *Haida* from 1956 to 1958. "She was different that she had been in wartime, of course, and it was a bit more comfortable."

Haida was laid down on September 29, 1941, by Vickers Armstrong Ltd. at Newcastle-on-Tyne, England. She was launched August 25 the following year, entering service with the Royal Canadian Navy one year and five days later.

She is now one of only three wartime Canadian ships still in existence. She lies in a man-made lagoon in Toronto, next to the provincial government's tourism showcase, Ontario Place. The ship is open to the public in the warm weather, and is also used extensively by the Royal Canadian Sea Cadets, a nation-wide youth movement supported by the Navy League of Canada and Department of National Defence.

It is fitting that her final berth is offshore from this inland city, because a publicity tour of the Great Lakes was in fact her last operation before she was paid off. And while she was in Toronto, taking reporters, veterans and school groups on tours, she was visited by six former crewmembers calling themselves the Preserve Haida Organization, later known as Haida Inc. They began a movement to purchase her for preservation, and the result of their efforts now sits proudly afloat, teaching new generations about life on the wartime seas.

Haida's life on those wartime seas was a charmed one, but it was by no means easy. She was the fourth of the Tribal class to join the Canadian fleet, preceded by *Iroquois*, *Huron* and *Athabaskan*. Problems with design discovered in two of the earlier vessels were corrected in *Haida*, and she sailed with strengthened upper decks and other modifications.

She was in fact specifically designed not as a submarine killer, but for attacks on surface vessels. Lean and powerful, she has been described by some writers as a "pocket cruiser," sporting six 4.7 inch guns in twin mounts, two 4-inch high-angle guns, six Oerlikons, a multi-barrel two-pounder pom-pom, four torpedo tubes and 45 depth charges. She is 377 feet long, 37 feet wide, and displaced 3,000 tons in wartime configuration. Her first crew of 18 officers and 230 men was captained by Commander Harry G. DeWolf, a regular navy officer.

After her trials, *Haida* joined the escort force for the Murmansk convoy runs. Although she saw little action in this role, she was with her sisters *Huron* and *Iroquois* providing close escort for convoy JW-55B on Christmas Day, 1943, when Grand Admiral Karl Doenitz decided that it was time to use one of his few remaining capital ships to wreak destruction on the Russian life-line. The battle cruiser *Scharnhorst* was ordered out of her hiding place on the Norwegian coast, and she weighed anchor at 7 p.m., escorted by the German 4th Destroyer Flotilla.

Unknown to Doenitz, the convoy was also being escorted by Force 1, consisting of three British cruisers, *Belfast, Norfolk* and *Sheffield*. Also close by was Force 2, the Royal Navy battleship *Duke of York*, the cruiser *Jamaica*, and a screen of British and Norwegian destroyers.

Twice the *Scharnhorst* attempted to close the convoy and was driven off by the guns of Force 1. DeWolf and his officers on *Haida's* open bridge could only watch tensely as the gunfire flickered on the horizon.

As *Scharnhorst* fled, she was met by Force 2, and went down, flag flying, under the guns of HMS *Duke of York*. Convoy JW-

55B sailed safely on to Kola Inlet, although *Haida's* guns opened fire to drive off attacking aircraft, and depth charges were dropped on submarine contacts.

In early 1944, *Haida* left the Russian convoys and joined the 10th Destroyer Flotilla based at Plymouth. Here, in the Channel, she began the most exciting period of her life. And it was here, in late April, that she lost a sister.

On April 26th, *Haida*, *Huron*, *Athabaskan* and *Ashanti*, with the British cruiser *Black Prince*, made radar contact with a force of German destroyers off the French coast. A few minutes after 2 a.m. *Black Prince* signalled contact with several enemy ships bearing 081 degrees at seven miles. For the next 15 minutes, it was a stern chase at high speed, and then *Black Prince* illuminated with star shell.

A few minutes later *Haida* and *Athabaskan* opened fire at 10,900 yards, joined shortly by fire from *Black Prince*.

The enemy force consisted of three Elbing-class destroyers, T-29, T-24 and T-27. They made smoke and launched torpedos in an attempt to slow down or drive off their attackers. At 2:48 the B turret on *Black Prince* failed, and the cruiser was forced to haul off to seaward, leaving Harry DeWolf and *Haida* in command.

It was now an equal fight, three against three, but the British and Canadian destroyers were also taking fire from German shore batteries on the French coast. As the running fight moved through the Channel, the fire from shore died away.

Suddenly, at 3:25 a.m., *Haida* spotted T-29, the German flotilla leader, attempting to escape through smoke to the westward. *Haida* and *Athabaskan* altered course to intercept, and fire was opened at 4,000 yards. The enemy vessel was hit, and was soon burning fiercely.

The Canadian ships launched torpedoes, but with no apparent effect. Harry DeWolf closed to within 1,000 yards and opened fire with his guns, and suddenly the German came to life, firing back with short-range weapons. She was burning from stem to stern, but was still on an even keel.

Haida withdrew to allow *Ashanti* and *Huron* to close, and under this withering fire the enemy destroyer began to go down. The flotilla commander, the ship's captain, and most of T-29's crew were lost.

It was the first time the Royal Canadian Navy had sunk an enemy destroyer in surface action.

After the elation . . . came the tragedy. At 3 a.m. on the 29th of April, *Haida* and *Athabaskan* were on patrol off the Isle of Ushant, near the French coast. They were ordered to search for two of the German destroyers they had engaged previously, T-27 and T-24, both of which had been damaged in the earlier engagement. At about 3:30 a.m. first *Athabaskan* and then *Haida* obtained radar contacts, and altered course to close. The two enemy vessels were on their way from St. Malo to Brest for repairs.

Shortly after 4 a.m., at 7,300 yards range, *Haida* signalled to her sister to engage, and fired a star shell. Both ships began to roll to the recoil of their salvos. The enemy vessels made smoke and veered eastward, toward the French coast.

Shortly after the Canadian ships had turned towards their targets, thus trying to narrow their silhouettes against torpedo attack, *Athabaskan* shuddered, slowed, and came to a halt. She had been struck by a single fish astern. Her captain, Lieutenant-Commander J.H. Stubbs, ordered the boats swung out. Meanwhile, *Haida* was left to shoot it out with the two German tin cans.

Suddenly there was an explosion aboard *Athabaskan*, and she heeled, going down by the stern until her stem was pointing almost straight up. She poised there a moment, and then slid down, taking her captain and 128 others with her.

Haida was fighting for her life. She had made hits on T-24, which broke away to the eastward, while T-27 made a dash for the French coast, *Haida* in hot pursuit. By 4:30, ablaze from stem to stern and clearly visible to the gunners aboard the Canadian destroyer, T-27 beached off Pontusval. She would fight no more.

DeWolfe ordered *Haida's* helm put over, and she raced to succor the survivors from her sister ship. All that was left of

Athabaskan was an oil slick, debris, and struggling men.

T-24, meanwhile, had escaped, and put in at Morlaix. A week later, a flotilla of motor torpedo boats were sent to complete the destruction of the grounded T-27. She was found to be so badly damaged that only one fish was put into her.

As *Haida* came up on the site of the sinking of *Athabaskan*, her motor cutter and two other boats were lowered, and scramble nets put out. In all, she rescued 42 survivors, but left as dawn broke to avoid becoming a victim herself. Two of *Haida's* sailors were swept off the scramble nets as DeWolfe ordered full speed, and the motor cutter, manned by three volunteers, was left behind.

Haida entered Plymouth harbour around breakfast time, her decks slick with oil from the *Athabaskan* survivors, her battle ensign flying from the yardarm. It was a grim victory, as ship after ship saluted her as she made her way slowly to her berth.

Meanwhile, 100 miles offshore, the volunteer crew of the motor cutter were engaged in a sea saga of their own. They had somehow found and picked up the two *Haida* men swept off the scramble nets, and had also saved six more men from *Athabaskan*. Chased by a German minesweeper, buzzed by enemy aircraft, and struggling with a malfunctioning engine, they nonetheless made their way safely to a rendezvous with a rescue launch near Penzance.

The rest of the *Athabaskan* survivors, 83 men clinging to Carley floats, were picked up by German minesweepers and spent the rest of the war as prisoners.

When the Allied invasion of the Normandy beaches began on June 6, 1944, *Haida* had to content herself with routine patrolling in the Channel, protecting the convoy lanes leading to the beachhead. Three days later, in the early morning hours of June 9, *Haida* was making a sweep in concert with HMCS *Huron* when she obtained a firm radar contact at six miles. They closed to within a mile, believing that it might be HMS *Tartar*, crippled in an earlier action. But their light signals brought only an unintelligible reply.

Suddenly, the mystery ship made smoke and sped away. It

was the German Narvik-class destroyer Z-32, larger and faster than the Tribals. At 31 knots, she began to open the range, but was running out of sea room, hemmed in as she was by an Allied minefield. But the German captain took the risk, and plunged eastwards toward Cherbourg. The Tribal sisters altered away to skirt the minefield, and radar contact was lost.

Twenty minutes later the enemy vessel was detected, pounding away at 31 knots. The Canadians maintained a parallel course, and suddenly the German destroyer veered closer.

A running fight developed as the three ships bore down on the rocky shoals off the French coast, going like spit and firing like fury, star shell and main armament blazing away. One German salvo landed 50 feet off *Haida's* bow, while some hits were obtained on the Narvik-class ship, cutting its speed.

Suddenly, shortly after 5 a.m., the German destroyer fetched up on the rocks off Ile de Bas. Fires broke out, and in the glow *Haida* and *Huron* steered away from Plymouth.

Haida joined the official ranks of the U-boat killers on June 24. She was ten miles north-northwest of Ushant, under a cloudless blue sky, when lookouts spotted a Liberator bomber dropping depth-charges on a surfaced U-boat about five miles astern. The aircraft, flown by a Free Czech crew, then dropped a smoke marker as the submarine dived.

This was U-971, which had been under repeated air attack since leaving her base in Norway two weeks earlier. Her captain took her to the bottom, hoping to lie doggo amidst the wrecks on the Channel floor.

Haida and the RN destroyer *Eskimo* approached slowly in line abreast, conducting a sound search. The first attack was made at 4:30 p.m. and depth charges were dropped for two hours, springing leaks in the U-boat's hull. With his crew standing ankle deep in water, her skipper decided to fight it out on the surface, and blew ballast.

As soon as the conning tower broke surface, *Haida's* "B" turret opened up and scored hits. Soon, the Germans were jumping into the water as the sub sank beneath them. The two destroyers picked up 53 from a crew of 54, landing them later at Plymouth.

DeWolfe then received a message from HMS *Black Prince*: "Narviks, Elbings and submarines all seem to come alike."

Haida saw more action throughout the rest of the war, and arrived triumphantly back in Canada on June 10, 1945. She was undergoing refit for the Pacific Theatre when Japan surrendered. And so she passed into reserve, along with many other fighting ships.

Haida was re-activated in 1947, and underwent a trouble-plagued fitting out and working up period. On November 17, 1949, under Lieutenant-Commander E.T.G. Madgwick, she was sent, along with the aircraft carrier HMCS *Magnificent*, into heavy weather near Bermuda to search for the crew of a downed U.S. B-29 bomber.

With seas breaking over the carrier's deck as she was landing aircraft on, *Haida* spotted a circling B-17 and moved in. Rolling at one point to 42 degrees, she closed to a life-raft holding the downed bomber's crew, and her whaler was lowered to leeward. Shortly, the wet but thankful airman were hauled aboard, and *Haida* made way to rejoin the carrier.

The rescue brought letters of congratulation, and a certificate for the ship's company:

> Whereas it has been brought to the attention of the nominating committee that the Officers and Crew of the Destroyer *Haida* have been outstanding in their field for many years, and rescued the shipwrecked crew of a B-29 plane whose co-pilot was a Texan; and whereas they would likely bring further honors to the State of Texas, they are hereby made Honorary Texans.

She spent the next two years in reserve, undergoing conversion to pure anti-submarine role. Squid anti-submarine mortars were fitted on her after deck, replacing one of the gun mounts. She was recommissioned on March 15, 1952, becoming the first Canadian warship to commission under the sovereignty of a queen. Her new skipper was Commander Dunn Lantier, survivor of the *Athabaskan* sinking. He had spent the final year of the war as a prisoner.

Now it was time to go to war again . .. this time in Korean waters. *Haida* reached Japan on November 12, 1952, having stopped over at Pearl Harbour en route. The following week she sailed to join the United Nations ships operating off Korea. By this time, the fighting on land had reached a stalemate, and naval forces were mainly being used for blockade and escort duties. On December 6, *Haida* was on station off the east coast of the peninsula, in company with USS *Moore*, when they were called upon for fire support for the landing of supplies on the island of Yong Do. Once again, her guns blazed forth, and hits were observed on a factory and marshalling yards at Songjin. Turning away, *Haida* came under fire from enemy shore batteries, which were then engaged and silenced by her after 3-inch 50 (3.5 inch) armament.

In the next two weeks, *Haida* joined the "Train Busters Club," shooting up Communist supply trains which tried to run across exposed stretches of track between tunnels under cover of darkness.

In June 1953, *Haida* sailed for home, making her first circumnavigation of the globe and reaching Halifax in July. After several weeks of refit, she sailed again for Korean waters, reaching the Far East February 5, 1954. After the armistice was signed in July, she maintained patrols along the coast until ordered home again in September. Once again, she completed a globe-circling cruise, and took up her peacetime Canadian fleet duties.

One of these duties, in the spring of 1956, was especially poignant. As *Haida* lay in port in Montreal, pipes were sounded, and the chief of the naval staff, Vice-Admiral Harry G. DeWolf, Commander of the British Empire, Distinguished Service Order, Distinguished Service Cross, stepped aboard.

By the early 1960s, she was showing signs of advanced age. In December 1962, when full-power trials were attempted, several defective bearings were discovered both in the main engines and in the boiler room fans. After she returned to the dockyard, more defects were discovered, keeping her alongside for a further two months.

By this time, her paying off date had already been announced, and in early summer 1963, she began preparations for her final operation, a goodwill tour of the Great Lakes. And it was at this time that the first steps were taken to preserve her.

Now she floats quietly and majestically in sweet water, visited each year by thousands. On weekends, Sea Cadets swarm aboard for training, and each summer her guns fire again in accompaniment to the "1812 Overture" played by the Toronto Symphony Orchestra at Ontario Place, just across the lagoon.

But there is another annual tradition that is also observed, solemnly and silently by an ever-dwindling number of ageing men. They gather aboard her in late April, and services are conducted to commemorate the loss of her sister Tribal, HMCS *Athabaskan*, and all those who went down with her.

Her battle honors are as follows:

Arctic	1943-1945
English Channel	1944
Normandy	1944
Biscay	1944
Korea	1952-53

HMCS *Haida* is open to the public each year from May to September. Hours are 10 a.m. to 7 p.m. weekdays, 10 a.m. to 8 p.m. weekends. Further information can be obtained by writing to:

HMCS *Haida*
Ontario Place
944 Lakeshore Blvd. W.
Toronto, Ontario
CANADA M6K 3B9

Canada's Last Carrier

In 1967, as Canada's armed forces were undergoing the traumatic process of being blended into one organization with a common green uniform, the navy at least could take heart that its only major warship, the light fleet carrier HMCS *Bonaventure*, would be around for some time to come. The "Bonnie" had just come out of an expensive and extensive 16-month refit, $11 million worth, designed to extend her operational life well into the next decade, and perhaps beyond. Then, just three years later, inexplicably and in seeming haste, the decision was made to scrap her. Today, the *Bonaventure* is just a memory for those who served aboard her and flew aircraft from her decks. She is thus an important part of modern Canadian naval history.

During the Second World War, Royal Canadian Navy pilots mostly flew combat missions from the decks of British carriers. One of them, Robert Hampton "Hammy" Gray, won the Victoria Cross posthumously by carrying out a daring bombing attack on a Japanese destroyer days before hostilities in the Pacific ended. Oddly enough, Canadians manned the two small British carriers *Nabob* and *Puncher*, while flying off British Fleet Air Arms aircrews.

After the war, Canada obtained the use of HMS *Warrior* the fledgling Canadian naval air arm, and in 1948 she was replaced by HMCS *Magnificent*. However, by the 1950s, it became obvious that major refitting would have to be done if the "Maggie" was to handle jets. The other option was to acquire a completely Canadian vessel, and have her built to specifications.

Enter HMS *Powerful*, a Majestic-class carrier laid down November 27, 1943, as a sister ship to *Magnificent*. Her hull was launched on February 27, 1945, but when the war ended, work was suspended in May of 1946. In 1952, Canada approached the

British Admiralty with an offer to purchase the ship. She was redesigned by Harland and Wolff to include the most up-to-date Royal Navy innovations, including an angled and strengthened flight deck, improved arrester gear, the mirror landing aid system, and the lastest British-designed steam catapult, capable of launching jets and heavier types of aircraft. These changes all added to safety and flexibility.

She was commissioned on January 17, 1957, at Belfast, and was christened *Bonaventure*, for the island off the Gaspe Peninsula in the Gulf of St. Lawrence named in 1534 by explorer Jacques Cartier. She was the first carrier owned outright by Canada, but few could have realized that she would be the only one, and the last aircraft carrier the fleet would see.

After months of trials and workups, she arrived in Halifax, that great wartime convoy port, on June 26, in heavy fog. Briefing notes prepared by naval headquarters staff in 1955 pointed up the need for naval aviation to keep abreast of the latest developments in anti-submarine warfare, which has traditionally been the role of Canadian sailors since the days of the North Atlantic wolfpacks:

> The continuous modernization of Canadian Naval Aviation, and in fact, of the RCN as a whole, is most essential for the protection of our coasts and of the Atlantic lifeline. Our potential enemy has an estimated 500 submarines, in addition to 4,000 shore based naval aircraft. It is hard to believe that this fleet is being built up without an eye to the possibility of attacking our vital sea communications.

The Royal Canadian Navy, and the Canadian Armed Forces of today, have always been firmly part of an alliance. Canada was one of the driving forces behind the formation of NATO, and its ships to this day participate in exercises with those of American, British and other Commonwealth navies. The staff paper of 1955 notes:

The RCN should not be regarded as a single force by itself. It is part of what could almost be described as a huge international fleet under NATO, each section of that fleet having a particular job to do.

Bonaventure's job, then, was to provide aviation for the anti-submarine role. She was soon carrying both Banshee jet fighters as well as Sea King helicopters for surveillance and ASW work. The Trackers were retired from service only in 1990, after filling a variety of roles including fisheries patrol and search-and-rescue. The venerable Sea Kings are still in service, flying from land bases and from flight decks of destroyers. They did yeoman service during the Gulf War in intercepting maritime traffic bound for Iraq.

In 1958 an energetic officer named Bill Landymore, later to become rear-admiral, took command. At this time, flying was still being done according to wartime procedures, and was largely restricted to daylight hours. Aircraft might well launch in the darkness before dawn, but it was preferable to have them all recovered before sunset. Landymore challenged his flyers, pointing out that the potential enemy didn't quit work at night, so why should they?

The outcome of the challenge was something called SUSTOPS, for sustained operations. After procedures were worked out and additional aircrews provided to lessen fatigue, *Bonaventure* was able to keep four Trackers airborne day or night. An area 200 miles square could be kept saturated with Trackers and helicopters around the clock. SUSTOPS became a standard other navies tried to emulate. "She was a really unique ship, and quite capable of flying off when others stood down," recalls Lieutenant-Commander Dick Pepper, who flew "backseat" in Trackers and later as a co-pilot in helicopters off the carrier. "It was a terrifying experience when you were 'catted' off in the middle of the night, especially in stormy weather."

The Tracker figures in one of the more hair-raising if

somewhat comedic episodes in *Bonaventure's* life. In the mid-60s, the first of six airborne Trackers was landing on when one wheel went over the side, breaking open the fuselage and dumping the aircrew into the sea. The escort destroyer steaming on her quarter moved in to pick up the four men in the water. However, as she was lowering a whaleboat, things came unglued, and the bow of the whaler went into the water first, tipping its crew into the sea as well. The Bonnie's Captain, Bob Timbrell, remembers:

> So now we had four of my airmen in the water, plus the full whaler crew. The destroyer then started to throw heaving lines to pull out their whaler crew. They were still manoeuvring, and the heaving lines got sucked up into the intakes and the circulating water pumps, which resulted in the destroyer becoming immobile.

Timbrell, who retired as a rear-admiral, was still faced with the problem of recovering the remaining five aircraft in the early morning darkness. He was steaming at 20 knots into the wind, and his planeguard escort was dead in the water. What to do? "I told the destroyer to have its second boat ready. We then circled the destroyer five times. Each time we got into the wind, we recovered one Tracker. If there was a problem, it would be close to the destroyer." There were no further problems, and the soggy airmen and sailors were rescued safe and sound. Timbrell, and other accounts of this incident, leave the hapless destroyer nameless, probably for her own good.

A more sobering and dramatic episode occurred in September of 1962. *Bonaventure* and her destroyer escort, HMCS *Athabaskan*, were steaming to join a NATO exercise when she received orders to proceed at speed to a point 500 nautical miles of the coast of Ireland. A Flying Tiger Airlines Super Constellation with 76 people aboard had suffered engine failure, and had ditched. From first light on September 24th, *Bonaventure* kept her aircraft aloft, searching for signs of survivors. At noon, they intercepted the Swiss ship *Celerina*, which had picked up 48 people from a raft in the early morning hours. Four badly-injured survivors were transferred by helicopter to the carrier for medical treatment. The aerial search continued for several more hours, but no more survivors were found.

In 1964 *Bonaventure* took part in what was to become one of the longest United Nations peacekeeping operations in history. In that year, the simmering hatreds between Greek and Turkish populations on the island of Cyprus were threatening to erupt into open warfare. Canada agreed to send a force of men and equipment, and the aircraft carrier was ordered home from Gibraltar where she was taking part in NATO exercises. In Halifax, she was loaded with army vehicles and stores, and then was turned into a troopship as the soldiers came aboard. She reached Famagusta on March 30th and immediately began landing the peacekeeping force. Canada has had troops patrolling between the factions on the Mediterranean Island ever since.

No amount of refitting or redesign could alter the fact that *Bonaventure* had been built for the Second World War, to Royal Navy specifications of the 1940s including hammocks and messdecks. Postwar sailoring called for bunks and dining halls, and this resulted in cramped lower deck spaces for everyone. Even chief petty officers were stacked four high. As new equipment was fitted to keep up with technological progress, so space became tighter and tighter. Her crew froze in the winter and cooked in hot weather, but there was tremendous morale and pride in a job well done. She was always described as a happy and efficient ship. One of the more enduring and memorable traditions was that of the children's party, used as a calling card in foreign ports. Invitations were sent out in advance, to poor and handicapped kids, and once "Bonnie" was alongside the crew would rig up miniature merry-go-rounds, and a train pulled by one of the flight deck tractors. There would be clowns and pirates, races on the flight deck, and tons and tons of ice cream, soft drinks and hamburgers. It was a way for the crew, many of whom missed their own children while on long voyages, to give a little joy to their tiny guests.

Although she was laid down at 16,000 tons, when loaded *Bonaventure* was rated at 20,000 tons. With a top speed of 22 knots, she was way below what the U.S. Navy considered acceptable, and American flyers would not even consider operating jets from a flight deck only 700 feet long. In 1966, *Bonaventure* was due for a mid-life refit. She was too old, too slow and too crowded. The projected cost for the refit was $11 million, but it eventually ran up to $17 million, with many questions asked in Parliament and scurrilous cartoons in the press. America offered to sell Canada updated Essex-

class carriers for the bargain -basement price of $4 million apiece. But the government realized that a bigger ship would mean more expense in the long run. Still, for what was eventually spent on the refit, they could have bought four Essex carriers, and had change left over.

Despite tight money, combined Canadian and American ingenuity helped baffle the Royal Navy during an exercise in 1963. Jezebel was a new submarine detection and identification system developed by both countries in which a sonobuoy picked up low-frequency sound and transmitted it to an aircraft overhead to be analyzed. The problem with it was that the equipment was so large it could only be carried in shore-based aircraft. However, the squadron electronics officer aboard *Bonaventure*, Gary Crosswell, jury-rigged small relay stations using Heathkit parts. These were installed in the Trackers and could be used to relay the Jezebel data direct to the carrier. As a result, excellent results were obtained against British target subs during the exercise, and the Canadians couldn't tell the British how they were doing it because the Americans hadn't cleared Jezebel for anyone else.

Dick Ouellette, who served aboard as a Tracker co-pilot in 1967-68, remembers passing through a hurricane in December, 1968 with winds up to 100 knots. "The rollers were breaking right over the flight deck," he remembers. "The destroyers with us looked like submarines. The old hammocks would have been better than bunks, because we kept rolling out of our bunks." Several crew members were slightly injured, and damage was done to deck fittings. The breakwater was torn loose and driven astern, opening a hole in the forecastle through which water poured. Quick shoring action by damage control teams prevented serious harm.

In an average year the small Canadian carrier handled 2,500 deck landings and steamed the equivalent of twice around the world, about 42,000 nautical miles. She was away from Halifax more than 200 days a year, be it winter training in the Caribbean or NATO exercises in the deadly North Atlantic. She quickly gained the reputation of staying on station long after larger carriers had suspended operations due to heavy weather.

When Paul Hellyer became minister of national defence in the government of Lester Pearson in 1964, he paid a visit to the "Bonnie" to watch her in action. Captain Bob Timbrell was in command, and he and his aviators talked the politician into donning a life vest and taking the co-pilot's seat for a catapult Tracker launch. In his definitive book *The Sea is at Our Gates* Commander Tony German describes what followed:

> The pilot, he (Hellyer) was assured would be the most experienced in the navy. When the pilot appeared, white of hair, patch over one eye, he tottered across the flight deck with a cane and poked blearily at the aircraft's innards. The deck crew lifted him . . . reverently into his seat. If naval aviators have a failing, it is perhaps in thinking everyone has their slapstick sense of humor. In fact, they were dealing with a man who had no sense of humor at all.

Within five years, Hellyer had rammed the three services into a blender, producing the Canadian Armed Forces in a common green uniform. The *Bonaventure* was gone, the Trackers were operating from shore bases, and Canadian naval aviation was all but finished.

Bonaventure made her last entrance into Halifax as an operational carrier in December, 1969. Lieutenant-Commander J.B. "Pop" Fotheringham, who had made the first deck landing on *Bonaventure*, also made the last on December 12.

Four Trackers from VS880 remained aboard for a final flypast, but at the last minute the steam catapult failed. However, in order to spare them the ignominy of being hauled over the side onto a barge, Captain Jim Cutts drove the carrier around Bedford Basin like a destroyer, full revs on and helm hard over. With 17 knots of winds over the deck and engines howling, the last four Trackers roared aloft.

After she was paid off and stripped of all useable military equipment, *Bonaventure* was put up for sale. Mitsui of Japan bought her, and in company with Tung-Cheng Iron and Steel Works of Taiwan, she was cut to pieces in the southern Taiwanese port of Kaohsiung. "There were 13 years of life left in her when she was scrapped," maintains Vice-Admiral Harry Porter, her skipper in 1965 to 1966. "Scrapping the *Bonaventure* was, pretty well, the death knell for fixed wing aviation in the navy."

The Sea King helicopters continue to fly today from shore bases and from the flight decks of Canada's destroyers. The *Bonaventure's* wartime-vintage Bofors guns were transferred to army use, and were employed by 4 Canadian Mechanized Brigade Group in Europe to defend the airfields at Lahr and Baden used by CF-104 Starfighters and then by CF-18s. After their replacement with a new air defence system, they were slated for storage or museums, but the Gulf conflict saw them once again at sea, hastily jury-rigged to the three ships of Canada's task group. The navy is still not through with them, as they are to be mounted aboard a new class of mine counter-measures vessels to be manned by naval reservists.

HMCS *Bonaventure*

Specifications

20,000-ton Majestic class light fleet carrier
- **Length:** ....720 feet
- **Beam:** ....80 feet
- **Draught:** ......25 feet
- **Flight deck:** ..700 feet by 112 feet
- **Armament:** ..Four Three-inch /50 twin mounts (Eight guns)
  Eight Bofors 40-mm anti-aircraft guns
  Four saluting guns
- **Aircraft:** ....34 total
- **Machinery and powerplant:** Parsons single-reduction geared turbines driving twin shafts. 42,000 shaft horsepower at top rated speed of 24 knots. Four Admiralty three-drum boilers developing 350 pounds per square inch pressure.
- **Crew:** ....1,370 at wartime strength.

The Corvettes

They were built in their hundreds, cheap and nasties, with tubby little hulls and cramped crew spaces. Those who sailed in them claimed they would roll on wet grass, but they saved the day during those dark early years of the Battle of the Atlantic, fussing around the convoys like sheepdogs and racing to do battle with the U-boat wolf packs.

They were the corvettes, based on a British Admiralty design, adapted from a whale catcher called the Southern Pride. She had been built by Smith's Dock Company at Southbank on the Tees, and the modified specifications for "Patrol Vessel - Whaler Type" called for a length of 205 feet, a beam of 33 feet, and a draught of 15 feet.

The design was accepted by the Admiralty as part of a plan to put Britain on a war footing by 1940. Close escort vessels would obviously be needed, and existing warships took too long to build. Contracts for the first corvettes were awarded in February, 1939, and as the world situation deteriorated in those last months of peace, the plans were changed and changed again, to increase tonnage and armament.

The design finally settled on 940 tons, still within the 205-foot overall length, with a complement of 47 all ranks.

Shortly after the outbreak of war, the Admiralty sent the Royal Canadian Navy a set of plans for a "look-see." Within 72 hours, a proposal was made that Canadian shipyards, which had never built anything longer than 100 feet, could mass-produce this type. At the time, it was thought that they would be used for coastal duties only.

As negotiations continued, Rear-Admiral Percy Nelles, the RCN's chief of staff, proposed that the vessels be called "corvettes," as he found "Patrol Vessel - Whaler Type" too much of a mouthful.

The corvette program wrought nothing short of a complete revolution in the Canadian shipbuilding industry. With a lack of materials, lack of yards, lack of skilled tradesmen, it seemed an almost impossible task. The initial program called for 64 corvettes, plus ten Bangor-class minesweepers, to be built and in service within two years.

The Canadian navy at that time had seven destroyers. By war's end, it would be the third-largest war fleet in the world, with a shipbuilding industry behind it that was second-to-none. And the corvette program was the catalyst that brought it about.

As well as those that saw service with the RN and RCN, 18 corvettes served with the United States Navy. They were called "gunboats" and bore the designation PG. The American corvettes were:

      USS Temptress PG62
      USS Surprise PG63
      USS Spry PG64
      USS Saucy PG65
      USS Restless PG66
      USS Ready PG67
      USS Impulse PG68
      USS Fury PG69
      USS Courage PG70
      USS Tenacity PG71
      USS Action PG86
      USS Alacrity PG87
      USS Brisk PG89
      USS Haste PG92
      USS Intensity PG93
      USS Might PG94
      USS Pert PG 95
      USS Prudent PG96

These American ships were fitted with home-grown armament and served throughout the war as coastal escorts. In all, 15 of these were built in Canada.

Corvettes had one great advantage over destroyers when it came to sinking submarines. The corvette had a turning circle of only 200 yards, half that of a U-boat. The corvette could therefore turn inside the submarine's circle, constantly getting ahead of it to drop depth charges.

The ultimate corvette development came in 1942, with the development of the River-class frigate. This vessel — 60 were built in Canada — was 300 feet long, with a top speed of 19 knots. Its big advantage was its endurance; it could cruise 7,200 miles at an economical 12 knots, twice the range of the early Flowers. The River-class were armed with two four-inch guns, bristled with anti-aircraft weapons, 150 depth charges and state-of the-art radar.

HMCS Sackville

A total of 111 corvettes were built in Canada for the Royal Canadian Navy, and 15 for the U.S. Navy. British yards built a further 136 which were used by the RN. Today, only one remains, the corvette *Sackville*.

Her Majesty's Canadian Ship *Sackville* was built by the Saint John Shipbuilding and Drydock Company in New Brunswick, and entered service in December 1941. Although a few early Canadian corvettes followed the British practice of being named after flowers, most carried the names of towns.

It is in Halifax, that great "eastern Canadian port" which played so great a role in the convoy saga, that *Sackville* rests today, carefully restored to her late wartime configuration, immaculate in Western Approaches blue and grey. She rides easily to her springs, alongside the Maritime Museum of the Atlantic, as visitors walk her decks and clamber through her cramped lower spaces, to marvel at the toughness and courage of those young men who went to sea in her 50 years ago.

The average corvette seaman in 1941 was 18 years old when he joined, and likely had never seen the sea. He came from a large industrial city or a small prairie farming town, the RCN's traditional recruiting base. In the engine room, the asdic compartment, and on the gunnery deck, he learned at sea how to fight the underwater enemy. Seldom getting out of foul-weather gear, he stood watch four hours on and, if he was lucky, eight hours off. And for all this was paid $1.85 a day.

Doug Finlay of Owen Sound, Ontario served as an engineroom artificer aboard the corvette *Baddeck*. He sums up living conditions aboard in one word: "Crowded."

"We patrolled mostly in the Channel and the Bay of Biscay, and part of the North Atlantic," he recalls. "When we got a ping we would go to action stations and throw our ashcans (depth charges) over the stern. We never brought a sub up, but there were probably a lot of fish killed."

In the stokehold it was Finlay's job to feed the three oil-burning furnaces that kept each of the two Scotch Marine boilers going. They were filled with 20 tons of superheated boiling water, and there was only one way out if something went wrong — straight up a narrow ladder to the weather deck.

"The Navy war was there right from the first day to the last," Finlay says. "Out there in the middle of the ocean, you feel like you're never going to get home. They tell you land is only two miles away — straight down. We were surprised when the submarines came up and surrendered, they were right underneath us."

Concerning the corvettes rough seagoing manner, Finlay tells what he says is his only "Salty tale" about the war. Many corvettes kept dogs as mascots, he says, and on *Baddeck*, the dog got so seasick it died. "We had to bury him at sea."

It is as a memorial to these men that *Sackville* was recovered and restored. She was dedicated on May 4, 1985, as the Canadian Naval Memorial.

She spent her operational career on the North Atlantic convoy runs, between St. John's, Newfoundland and Londonderry, Northern Ireland. While under the command of Lieutenant-Commander Alan Easton, and escorting a convoy on the night of 3-4 August, 1942, she engaged three U-boats in foggy weather within 36 hours. *Sackville* was covering another escort that was attempting to tow a damaged merchantman when the first contact was made. She sank a "milch cow" tanker with depth charges, slugged it out on the surface with another and hit it below the conning tower with her four-inch gun, and damaged yet another in a shallow depth charge attack.

For these actions, Lieutenant Easton received the Distinguished Service Cross, and other members of the crew were also decorated.

Towards the end of the war *Sackville* was used to train officers. Later, she was used to remove underwater harbour defences at Halifax, and Sydney, Nova Scotia. Then she went into reserve.

In 1953 *Sackville* was re-activated as a civilian-manned auxiliary, carrying out oceanography and fisheries research. Then she was taken over by the Defence Research Establishment (Atlantic) and ended her active career in the same field as she had started it — doing research for anti-submarine techniques.

By the early 1980s, those hoping to restore a corvette as a permanent exhibit were in trouble. It had been hoped to obtain one or two corvettes still in service with the Dominican Republic, the *Colon* (HMCS *La Chute*) and *Juan Alejandro* (HMCS *Louisbourg*). But they were driven ashore at Las Calderas Naval Base by a hurricane in 1979, and smashed beyond any hope of repair.

In 1982 the Canadian Naval Corvette Trust negotiated to obtain *Sackville*, although she no longer looked much like she had in her wartime days. She was loaded with more than 40 tons of additional superstructure, added during her postwar career, and this would have to be removed before anything else could be done.

In December 1982 *Sackville* was finally retired from the Navy, and the job of restoration began. Parts from the two Dominican ships were obtained, as were bits and pieces from around the world. The two-pounder Mark VIII pom-pom in her aft bandstand was obtained from the Irish navy, for example.

The refit, for such it was, was accomplished at a cost of close to $1 million dollars, much of it from private donations. On May 4, 1985, the government officially declared her to be the Canadian Naval Memorial, honoring all who have served in the naval service of Canada. In June of that year, she took part in the naval assembly at Bedford Basin marking 75 years of Canadian naval history.

In 1986, the group responsible for the ship was renamed the Canadian Naval Memorial Trust. Even as *Sackville* floats gently at her berth, many more thousands of dollars and much time and effort remain to be spent restoring her interior spaces.

Sackville is not alone at her berth. On the other side of the jetty lies the gleaming scientific survey vessel *Acadia*, which served in both World Wars and spent a total of 57 years as a working ship. She too is open to the public as part of the Maritime Museum of the Atlantic.